LINE BY LION
PUBLICATIONS

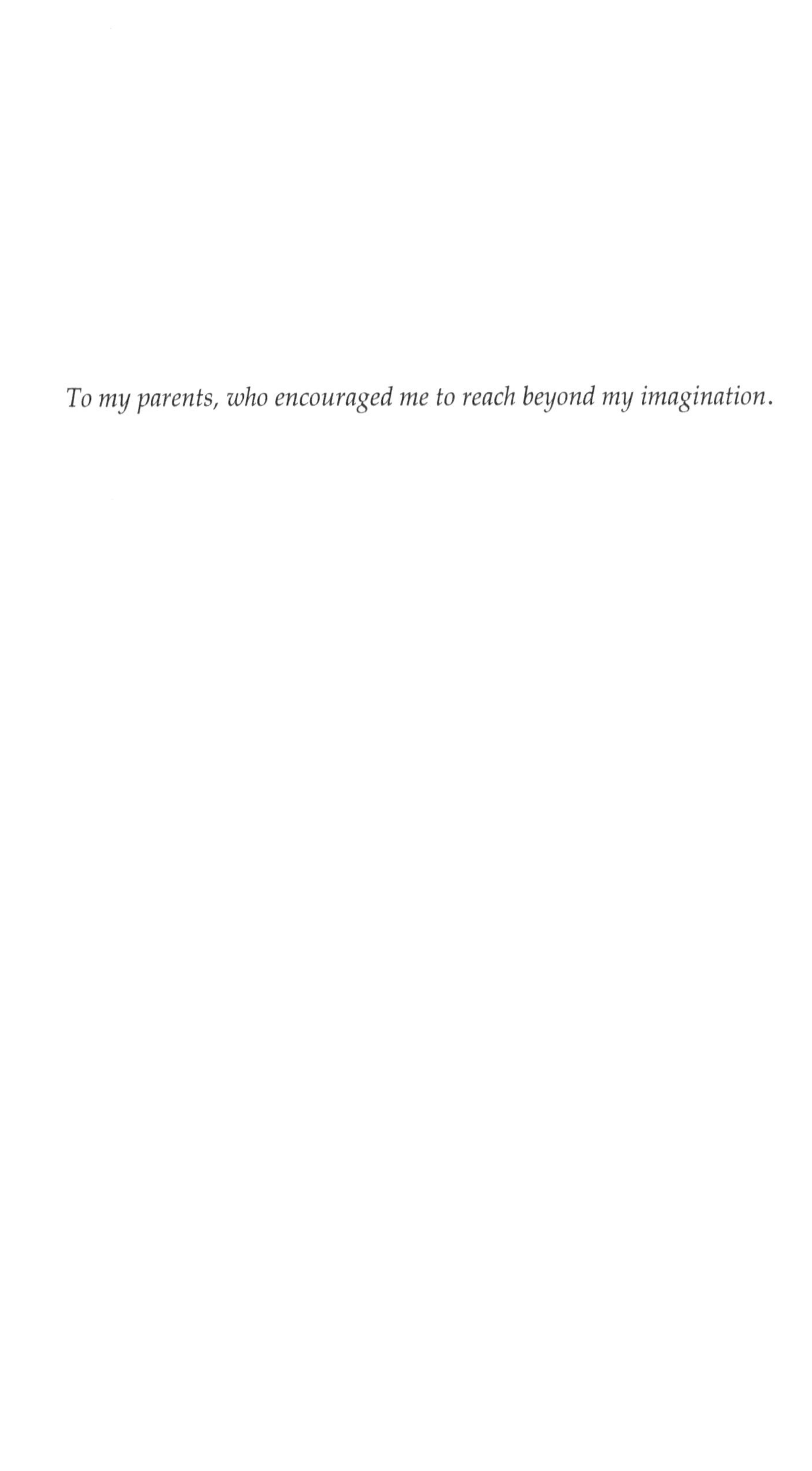

To my parents, who encouraged me to reach beyond my imagination.

CHAPTER
ONE

BANG. Crash. Crunch.

The sounds of metal and glass ring in my ears nearly every time I close my eyes.

The dead can speak. And I'm not talking zombies, vampires, the Lochness monster, although they do exist, I'm sure. I'm talking about ghosts. Full apparition, can walk through walls ghost.

My name is Thomas Crane, but most just call me Casper. That's right, Casper. The freak who speaks to the dead.

My dream caused me to awake with a stir. I sat up in my bed in a cold sweat. I looked around my room in my tiny apartment dreading the day ahead when a voice came from behind me.

"You were doing it again, you know."

I turned and saw a man, maybe in his early twenties, not much older than myself, who wore clothing you would probably see from a nineteen forties movie. White shirt, black pants and a matching vest, along with an old newsy hat with a rugged flap. He leaned over me and smiled a clean shaven grin at me.

Oh, and I could see through him. That part is kinda important.

"Hey, Vinny," I said, rolling my eyes, used to the same old morning routine.

"You were talking in your sleep, you goon. You're probably the reason half the dead can't get any rest," Vinny recited cheerfully.

He zipped over to my bedroom closet and opened it with an unsettling speed. Inside my closet was a mess of blacks and browns and several pairs of blue jeans. I was never known for my fashion sense. Unfortunately, buried in the back I could make out the grisly sleeve of an ugly blue polo, the picture of a half-eaten pretzel logo sticking out near the sleeve. My work uniform.

Possibly a bigger horror than half the things I have seen.

I tilted my head and looked up at the ceiling, trying to ignore my ghostly roommate's ramblings. "You know that car accident haunts me just as much as it haunts you, with as often as you complain about it," he continued.

I closed my eyes hard. Bang. Crash. Crunch. That was the last thing I'd heard before I awoke in a children's hospital. The doctors had told me that my father had died at the scene, and my mother had gone to another hospital. I think the loss of her husband made her go a little crazy because for reasons I never learned, I never did hear from her again. I sent her letter after letter, but I never received a thing. Not even a card for my birthday.

I was sent to an orphanage for damaged children. I spent seven long years there, and in that time I think I made one friend. And that friend was a twenty-something-year-old ghost named Vinny. This orphanage was old even when Vinny was here after he got dropped off because his parents couldn't afford food. Or drugs. It was a weird time.

After he failed to get adopted, he decided he would have fun terrorizing the staff on the grave shift. Vinny was 'the thing that goes bump in the night.' When I arrived at the orphanage, he had attempted to scare me with a series of shadow puppets on my bedroom wall followed by eerie sounds that kept me up. I think I was the one that scared him when I said "boo" while he was sneaking up on one of the young nurses that was on duty trying to catch a glimpse up her skirt. We became friends shortly after, our shenanigans getting us into trouble as I learned about the extent of my ghostly burden.

It was at this time the jokes began in the small Indiana southern town.

"Look, that boy is talking to an imaginary friend. Must be a ghost."

"Casper the ghost whisperer."

"No wonder he has never had a girlfriend, all he talks to is his 'boo!'" In hindsight it was never clever, but it still hurt all the same.

Vinny took care of me though. He explained that children, if exposed to a near-death experience, can sometimes interact with the dead and those that are deceased can contact those closest to them. I, for whatever reason, got this ability a thousand-fold. Ghosts are a tricky subject. They aim to wander this plane of existence because they have unfinished business. It's not like the stories you hear on the T.V. or the movies. Ghosts are normally harmless, just lost looking for answers.

Then there is Vinny. I think his task was to annoy me until I died myself.

"Come on chap, get up and get ready for work. You're already running late."

I looked at my clock on my bedside table but at some point in the night it had become unplugged. I forced the urge to not lay back down.

"Come on," Vinny urged. A ghostly tug at my covers caused them to fall to the floor.

"Someone has to make sure we are fed in this place."

I put my arm over my face, blocking out the light. "You're dead, Vinny. You don't need to eat," I said, wearily annoyed.

"You're right, and you take it for granted." Vinny whistled a sound that sounded like a broken windmill. "What I wouldn't give to know the taste of a steak sandwich again." He looked down at me with a parental stare. "You are a selfish lucky bastard."

I ignored him, yawned, and got out of bed clumsily. After getting my bearings I inched toward my open closet door and pulled out that blue polo. I eyed it with a cold stare. That pretzel logo was the symbol of defeat in my life as I knew it. I'd worked hard to get this small apartment. I'd spent the better part of two years at Twisted Joe's Snack Shack, despite applying everywhere else in the town mall, but unfortunately it was 'good ole' Joes that called me. You know how hard it is to be taken seriously with a giant pretzel on your chest?

I laid the uniform on the bed and made my way to the fridge. I opened it seeing the usual display of pizza boxes and energy drinks. I grabbed a can of sugary fluid and downed it fast. I needed the caffeine something fierce today,

"Vinny?" I called, crushing the can and throwing it into the trash. "Can you at least make yourself useful and start up a shower for me?" I turned around but the ghost was nowhere to be seen. Typical ghost move.

I was in the middle of heating up some frozen pizza from who knows how many nights ago when I heard the creak of a shower head and warm water coming out from the bathroom door. Good. My roommate can listen.

I scarfed down my tasteless meal and went to the bathroom prepared to wash off yesterday's grime and frowned. In the fogged up mirror an unseen finger was writing out letters in a slow manner. I read it aloud as each letter formed.

"F…U…C…K…" The writing got a bit faster as he continued, "You…" I said aloud finally. I stomped my feet aggressively toward the shower as I heard the squeak of a happy face being drawn onto frosted mirror,

"Oh Vinny," I said coolly. "You are lucky you're dead."

I grabbed a towel and began to wipe the mirror down as my reflection came back into view. I stared into the mirror for a minute, looking at my pathetic features. I was lean with shaggy dark shoulder-length hair, I was paler than a newspaper clipping. My dark eyes were sunken in from never enough sleep and my whole physique screamed sickly. I looked at my reflection again after a warm shower, but to my misfortune, there wasn't much of a difference.

I got dressed in my dumb uniform and exited my apartment, closing the door behind me harder than I intended. I sighed heavily, closing my eyes trying to relax.

Bang. Crash. Crunch.

Vinny was a jerk, but he was right. These dreams were an every night nightmare. The events of that accident had left me mentally scarred and forgetful. I could barely remember my parents' faces or their voices. It was all an illusion that I was forced to replay in my head every time I closed my eyes.

I turned and locked the door, pulling the handle hard to secure it. The doorframe squeaked. This building was old. Really old and was clearly haunted, given the roommate situation. It creaked eerily as I walked down the featureless hallway to the stairs. My apartment was on the third floor. It didn't have much of a view. I mean, if you look out my window, you can see the brick wall of the building next to it. But it was home.

I raced down the stairs feeling every step like I was going to fall through the wood to the sidewalk and looked out at my small, white Ford Focus. Hardly any miles on it, still in pretty decent shape. It's not like I went anywhere most nights, but it was my trusty steed all the same.

I flipped on the radio to listen to anything that was on to drown out last night's nightmare. The radio buzzed and my ears were nearly shattered by an impulse of static as I finally heard the last few bars of Bon Jovi's Living on a Prayer before a news report cut in: And with that our story goes out to yet another soul that was lost on St Bulivard street as another body was found dead at the scene. This has been the fourth death in an ongoing investiga-

I turned off the radio. The last thing my day needed was to add more death to the equation.

CHAPTER TWO

I drove my short drive to the mall. Entering through the slow automatic doors I walked past a dozen or so people wandering aimlessly. You know how I said zombies exist? I'm pretty sure even they are more lively than the clientele we have at this dump.

Not too many friendly faces so I figured I'd look the part as well. Not that I wanted to be here, mind you, but nothing helps a bad mood like spreading it around. My frown got even bigger as I neared the giant white tent in the middle of the mall in the most hideous attraction in the building. You can't miss it. It's right under the greased stained sign that says Twisted Joe's Snack Shack.

"You're late again," said a high pitched and annoying voice.

"Missed you too, Franklin," I replied.

A stout man with spiked red hair, maybe a foot shorter than me rounded the booth, wagging a plump finger at me. I braced myself knowing I was about to hear that shrill voice again. Franklin is my boss, and not a good one. Pretty sure the only reason he got the job is he applied two weeks before me. Franklin really knows how to brown-nose the right people, and to make matters worse, he was good at it.

"That's three times this week, Crane," he chanted, clearly enjoying knocking my ego down a few pegs. "What? Your imaginary friends keeping you up at night?"

"Oh if you only knew," I said between clenched teeth.

"That's gonna be a write up, Crane. I think you are going for a new record," he said grinning. Oh yeah, I knew he was enjoying this. "Now it's Thursday, and you know I have my meeting in the office today, and I want you behind the counter. That inventory is not going to sell itself."

By meeting he meant making out with his new girlfriend in his rusty pickup truck. Old girlfriend maybe? It was hard to keep track. This guy fancied himself as a player and somehow succeeded in being a lady's man, too. Trust me, this was an easy man to be annoyed by. I wanted to put him in his place but I was already in enough trouble as it was. I thought it best to keep my mouth shut.

"Whatever you say, Red. Have fun in your meeting. I hope she gives you the raise you deserve."

Hey, I said I knew better to keep my mouth shut. I never said I was good at it.

Franklin's face turned as red as his hair and his brow furrowed furiously. "You best watch it, Nosferatu. You are on very thin ice here, and all I gotta do is say one word." He followed it up by snatching a pretzel from the warmer and taking a huge bite inches from my face. "Don't give away free food. See? Now this is coming out of your paycheck."

He turned and stomped off munching violently at his snack. I slowly raised my middle finger in his direction. Vinny taught me well. "I hope your truck wife likes salt with her lipstick," I mumbled to myself.

I hopped behind the counter, laid out the fresh pretzels and leaned aggressively on the glass display table thinking about my past accomplishments. Thomas Casper Crane. No friends.

Horrible job. Dead roommate. Oh, and I can talk to spirits. Life pretty much sucks. I've met ghosts who don't feel as dead as I do.

About two and a half hours had gone by and all I had done was sold two bottles of water and gave directions to the nearest ATM. Franklin's meetings didn't normally last this long but I can't say I minded the silence. I had just started wiping the counters when I heard sirens blazing outside. It was a fairly quiet day in the mall so the sound echoed down every corridor. Curiosity got the better of me and I walked toward the door. Through the glass I could see several people huddled around something. Or someone. A pair of dirty black converse were sticking out from the crowd. There was a crimson flow of blood making its way along the ground between the bodies. The legs were not moving. I tried to get closer but the mall security stormed past me and ran outside, trying to get control of the crowd. Hollering and shouting followed as an ambulance entered the scene. I couldn't make out what anyone was saying but from what I gathered it was indeed an emergency.

I turned and started back toward the pretzel stand, barely beating Franklin there.

"You still haven't sold anything?" he questioned, his clothes wrinkled and untucked.

"In case you hadn't noticed, Red, there was a bit of an accident outside."

Red seemed to go out of his way to anger me. "And accidents make people hungry, do they not?"

"Umm, no?" I raised an eyebrow at his response. "Besides, it's time for me to go to break anyways."

"You will get a break when you do your job," he said sternly.

I had already hopped around the counter and began walking away. "Tell you what Red, you show me how it's done when I get back. You can tell me all about what you learn in your meetings."

I walked away quickly as Franklin cursed my name however he could. Weaving through the small crowds of people, all trying to get to the door, either wanting to know what happened or thinking they were in some sort of trouble. To be fair, I'd seen crazier stuff in this mall. Prime example, the maintenance guy with the curled mustache? Broke his neck falling off the annual Christmas tree about four years ago. He is a great guy.

I passed by the wall of shops with delicate ease. The smell of commerce in every step. There's the hunting shop. Over there the toy store. Did I mention the 23 clothes shops of brands no one can afford yet, somehow they stay in business? I never had much fashion sense. I mean look at me, I'm wearing a pretzel polo.

All these shops were just images in the wind. All except one. Shadow Hut. Shadow hut was one of those shops. You know the ones where people left looking like they belonged to some BDSM group. Chains on their belts, ripped up pants, more tattoos than skin, and black clothing. A LOT of black clothing.

So naturally, they felt like my kind of people.

But that isn't the reason that I personally came to this shop. In all honesty it's probably not the reason MOST came to this shop. They came to this shop for…

"That will be $27.95. Will you be using your Shadow Hut card?"

A voice of raspy angelic pleasure came from somewhere in the building. It was as if time suddenly stopped. That was the voice of the most mysterious and jaw-dropping woman I had ever known. That was the voice of Riley Blake.

I stood in the threshold of the front archway entering the shop looking inside to the strobe lights bouncing off the expensive T-shirts on the wall, the sound of music I couldn't quite understand coming from within. I took one step toward the door and looked down at my current wardrobe. I really wish I had my black leather jacket right about now. Cursed summer heat.

I removed my pretzel logo Polo from over my head revealing the plain black T-shirt I had underneath. Slinging the shirt over my shoulder I got up the courage to go inside, dodging a few patrons along the way. I stumbled over clothing racks that were way too close together, and then…there she was. Leaning over the counter like some kind of bombshell goth princess. She had long dark hair, black lipstick, and eyeshadow that made her naturally green eyes radiate. Dressed in a black, laced tank top with a bit too much cleavage shown (I tried not to stare) and her black vinyl pants clung to her tightly. I had to do a double take to make sure my jaw wasn't on the floor.

She looked up to hand a large bag of something or other to a tall bald man in a black T-shirt and blue jeans, a surprising contrast to the dark shadows on every corner (I mean, to be fair, I'm not one to talk but I work at the mall, sue me) and she caught me staring.

"Hey Susan, I'm going on break," Riley shouted while looking at me.

"Okay, Babe," a voice from somewhere in the back replied.

She stood up and grabbed a small bat-like purse from somewhere under the counter and came strolling up to me.

"You coming?" she said, her voice was even more angelic when it was directed at you.

"How do you know I'm not here to shop?" I said with a bashful smile.

She looked me up and down and rolled her eyes. "Nice try. Come on, I need a smoke." Riley Blake was one of the only people in my life I would actually consider a friend. I'd told her all about my ghostly connection and how I am able to talk to the dead. Whether she believed me or not, I couldn't say, but she definitely didn't treat me like a freak like the rest of them. I had shown a romantic interest when I first met her, and I think she knew it, but I had never pulled the trigger. My boss Franklin had tried and it may have been the happiest day of my life when her steel-toed heels kicked him in the balls so hard he cried.

Riley led me out a side door along the mall's eating court and we went outside. Just out of our peripheral you could still see the police cars and ambulance taking care of the victim of some tragic accident. Riley sat down on the curb and stared out at the incident.

"I heard it was a jumper," she said, pulling a pack of cigarettes from her back pocket. I'm surprised that pants that tight even have pockets.

"I haven't heard anything. I just saw the commotion from the pretzel stand." I sat next to her, staring down at my feet. "Makes for an interesting start to the work day."

Riley nodded slightly and lit up her cigarette, taking a long drag from it. She pulled it from her lips and blew smoke that I am fully convinced was purple. She handed her cigarette to me without saying a word. I took it from her. I'm not even a smoker. I think Riley knew this but I think it was her own twisted game to see what day I would snap. I just sat there looking at the burning joint.

There was a long moment of silence before Riley suddenly broke it. "So did you talk to him?"

I looked at her confused. "Talk to…?"

She pulled another cigarette and lit it with ease before turning her stare to me. "The jumper."

I looked down again. "No. I don't think it appropriate to seek them out like that."

She gave me a hard stare before returning to her smoke. "That's cool."

That's the thing about Riley. Whether she believed me or not about my ability, she never seemed to tease me about it. She legit seemed interested. I think she believed I believed it, and that made me feel very special.

Riley continued. "That's a shit way to go. Suicide I mean."

I nodded. "Since my ability I haven't met many who had lost their life to it. In the countless books I've read about ghosts and ectomancy, ghosts seem to stay on this plane of existence because they are seeking answers. They seek to protect, or haunt. They have unfinished business."

Riley remained fixated on that scene. "So when it's suicide, they feel they have already failed in their mission so they have no further reason to be here?"

I looked at the faltering still lit cigarette in my hand. "Makes about as much sense as I can get out of it."

Riley took another drag. "That sucks," she said dryly.

I nodded in approval. I'd been surrounded by death practically for as long as I could remember, but it never got any easier.

The crowd from the accident was starting to clean up. We watched as they pulled a man onto a stretcher and covered his face in a blanket before the ambulance sped off. No sirens. Riley stood up and flicked her cigarette on the ground, stomping it out. "Hey Thomas, do me a favor okay?"

I looked up at her intently. "Of course, Riley. Anything."

She looked me in the face for a long moment, almost as if she was studying me. Or maybe she was being cautious of how she worded the sentence that followed.

"When I die, don't let me stay stuck in this world."

I couldn't help but smile. "Trust me, I wouldn't keep you here."

Riley turned and put her thumbs in the elastic of her pants as she walked away. "I gotta get back to work. You take care of yourself, Casper."

I waved back, trying my hardest to play it cool. I stared at the cigarette still in my hand watching as the final embers burned to the filter.

CHAPTER
THREE

I stood up and brushed my hands off and looked one final time out at where the accident had been. There were about six people still at the scene. Two cops talking to an older man, I'd assume a witness to the jump, a woman, maybe in her early thirties, who was crying aggressively, a man who was cleaning up what had to be a grisly amount of blood, and another man with short brown hair, green hoodie, and light jeans. Probably not much older than the woman.

Curiosity got the better of me and I walked over to the scene. I stood next to the man in the green hoodie. The woman was crying so hysterically she didn't even notice me. The cops climbed into their car and drove away, as the woman dropped to her knees, kissed her fingers and lay them upon a freshly cleaned spot of gravel just outside the mall. She walked away paying no mind at all to me or the green hoodie man, her cries becoming softer and softer in the distance, leaving just the two of us.

It was all but silence aside from the traffic not too far away. I looked at the green hoodie man. There was pure sadness in his eyes. He was fixated on the clean spot in the road, his face emotionless. He seemed empty. Soulless.

"So why did you do it?" I finally asked.

The green hoodie man gave me an annoyed sideways glance and muttered, "Maybe I was a desperate man at the end of my rope? Why do you even care? I don't even know who you are."

I walked around and stood in front of him. "Because we both know that you regret it."

The green hooded man jumped in surprise as I talked directly to him. "Wait. WAIT. You can fucking SEE ME?"

I smiled that annoying smile. "I guess we are all full of surprises today, huh?"

The green hooded ghost's jaw dropped. "You…you can speak to me?"

I sighed. "Yes. I can speak to ghosts. Which, ding ding ding, is what you are. Surprise. Welcome to the afterlife."

Green-hooded ghost backed away from me. "Are…are you here to take me away?"

I laughed. "I promise you, I'm not some sort of angel or demon. Even I can't fully explain it, but here I am. If you were ever going to find a therapist in the afterlife, today is your lucky day." I swear I find it easier to talk to ghosts than the living. No wonder my social life is screwed. The green-hooded ghost seemed frightened so I tried to put on a friendly face. "Okay, fine. Let's start with your name."

The ghost looked timid, then muttered, "Simon."

"Simon. Good. Now tell me, Simon, do you know why you died?" I gritted my teeth. I had played ghost advocate way too many times. I know death is traumatic, I'm not a monster, but man do I hate it when they flip out. And Simon was on the verge of flipping.

Simon hesitated before looking up at the roof of the mall. He then looked back at me and then slowly craned his neck to look over at a large black truck sitting isolated in the middle of the parking lot. I couldn't see his face but I knew his eyes were filled with tears. I felt anger swelling inside me as I recognized the license plate of my boss's vehicle on the back.

"I…I followed her. I followed her from our home into the lot. I saw her get into that truck with that…small, red haired man. I thought maybe it was a friend, or a business partner or something but…" He turned to look back at me. "I couldn't live knowing she would hurt me."

Simon looked back at the spot where he had died just a little under an hour ago. "I thought she loved me, man." I wanted to cry myself. Not just because I had found out what an additional dirtbag my boss was. Not because I could feel the sadness in his voice, the love that was lost. But because I didn't know this ghost from Adam. I didn't know anything about him. This man really was at a loss, discovering his life's desperation, and I was the only hope he had. This man was in desperate need of a hug. And to make matters worse, I couldn't even do that.

Speaking to a ghost is one thing. Being able to touch one is a far greater power. I stood with him for a moment listening to his gentle sobs. "That was her, wasn't it? The woman who was here?"

Simon shook. I couldn't tell if he was holding back more tears or if he was nodding, but I felt I knew the answer all the same.

"She clearly had feelings for you. There was at least a love there once, yeah?" I said as tenderly as I could.

Simon looked up and smiled through his sadness. "Tsh, you keep saying had, was, like there is nothing I can do about it. I…I can get her back. I can…" He paused and for the first time since I'd seen this man, he seemed almost happy. "I can't do anything, can I?"

I looked at the sky for a moment. "I don't believe so, no. In my experience, that's not how the afterlife works. I think the best thing you can take away from this is, move on."

Simon laughed. "Move on? That easy? You want me to what? Just walk the world forever until I blow away in the wind? I want revenge."

I'll be honest, that thought did bring joy to me. I relished in the thought of Simon tormenting Franklin every day in his home, driving him crazy until the end of his time. In reality though, I wasn't fully sure how hauntings worked and I didn't want to mislead this poor ghost.

Besides, I wouldn't wish my greatest living enemy to live with that asshole.

"I am not sure revenge is the best course," I finally said. "You need to leave this parking lot and stop dwelling on this."

Simon looked out at the sun. "How long do I have?"

I shook my head. "It is different for every ghost I've met. But what else have you got to lose?" Simon took a few steps away from me before calling over his shoulder. "You know, your gift can't really help anyone, can it?"

I stared at him, feeling hurt, but I couldn't think of a comeback. In all this time I've had this ability, whatever had I really done with it? What could I do with it?

"…but you're right." he continued. "I can't stay here. I think I need to see what else is out there."

I turned, watching him walk away. "Good luck, Simon," I said, crossing my arms. Simon looked back at me one last time, looking down at my uniform.

"Maybe you should do the same."

Before I could respond, Simon took a few more steps out into the parking lot and vanished in a thin cloud of mist. I stared at it a moment before wiping a few tears from my eyes and walked inside, slowly. I really didn't want to see Franklin. I couldn't muster up enough thoughts of what I wanted to do to him. I felt bad for Simon. I wanted Franklin to pay for what he did, but what proof did I have?

"Yeah, the ghost of her true lover came to me and said that this man is a jerk," I said under my breath. Yeah. I'm sure that would go great in court.

My thoughts suddenly got interrupted as I came upon the pretzel stand. Sure enough, there was Franklin, munching down on a pretzel, liquid cheese falling down onto his messy shirt. (Seriously what did the girls see in this guy?)

He somehow heard me coming through his teeth chomping on barely cooked dough.

"Long enough break?" he asked angrily.

I didn't respond. I knew if I opened my mouth I was gonna say something aggressive. "Damn shame what happened outside, huh? Dumb bastard jumped I heard." "Oh, please stop talking," I thought to myself.

"Pity too. He was a good customer. Always got the cinnamon twist."

"Stop acting like you give a shit." I felt my fist growing hot with rage as I began cleaning up the counter.

"I will say the bastard sure had good taste in women. That girl of his? Whooo."

"OKAY, THAT'S IT." I felt my fingers wrap around a nearby rolling pin and I turned around. Next thing I knew my arm was cutting through the air with full force. The only thing stopping it was the sheer impact as wood collided with the back of Franklin's skull dropping him to the floor. He fell hard and turned around staring at me with a combination of fear and anger.

I dropped the roller with surprise. Where did that come from?

"What the hell is your problem, freak?" he shouted at me.

I jumped the counter and began storming off. "I don't feel well, I'm going home."

"Crane, you get back here, you hear me? Crane? You're fire…"

His yelling died down as I stormed off into the parking lot. Simon was right. I needed out, and I needed out now.

I ran for my Ford Focus and got into the driver's seat as fast as I could. I could already picture mall security getting Franklin's statement. They would be on my tail in no time. My hands hot with rage, I shifted the car in drive and got out of there, my car jumping a curb in the rush.

I got back into my subdivision in a blur. I parked the car checking my rearview mirror for anyone following me. No one. Good. I took a long deep breath before screaming as loud as I could. I banged my hands on the steering wheel and cursed loudly. I was no doubt fired. I had bills to pay and the rent was coming up fast and I'd just talked to a guy who killed himself over my boss's deception.

But the thing that my mind kept going back to was…what would Riley think? Would she be upset that I got fired? Would I ever see her again?

I got out of the car and slammed the door so hard the window actually cracked. I glared at it with an intense stare. Perfect. Just one more thing. I had to resist the urge to say "How could it possibly get any worse?" I still looked up at the sky expecting rain.

CHAPTER
FOUR

I decided to not go back inside my apartment just yet. It hadn't been too long since I'd left the mall and I'm pretty sure Franklin still had my address on file somewhere. I decided it would be better to go for a walk. I was still fuming with anger and I could still feel the force of that rolling pin in the palm of my hand. I shook my wrist to get rid of the memory.

It was late afternoon, so I figured I may as well go to my favorite bar on the street. Well, I call it a bar. It's actually an occult bookstore that just happens to sell alcohol of various literature names. The Open Page had been a staple in this town for well over a decade and I had been a long-time patron, as it was a short walk away from where I lived. The owner was an older man, long blonde hair and glasses by the name of Mr. Hunter. His large round glasses were always sitting on the bridge of his nose. I had to remind myself he had a beard most days because he always had a large book right up to his face.

"Thomas Crane." he called as I entered through the old wooden doors. "You're here much earlier than usual." He looked at the computer next to him. "And on a Thursday, too? What do I owe the pleasure?

I sat on a nearby bar stool, and looked behind the bar. No one was there. In fact Mr. Hunter was both the bartender and the salesman. He was currently behind the business desk eyeing me curiously.

"I'll have a Nevermore Ale please."

Mr. Hunter arose with the creak of his chair. He tried his best to hide his smile. "Awfully early for you isn't it? Ghost keeping you busy?"

I rolled my eyes. I knew he meant well, but unlike Riley, I knew this man didn't believe in my ability. He may own an occult bookstore, but I'm pretty sure it's because he saw dollar signs in the merchandise. Funny magic kits and wizard coloring books. He made more money with the booze anyways. But all the same I felt comfortable in the environment.

"Something like that," I responded.

Mr. Hunter opened a cooler from behind the bar and pulled out a bottle of amber liquid. He reached into his back pocket and retrieved a bottle opener. He popped the tab and the visual of icy mist filled the lid. My mouth watered in anticipation.

He sat the drink down in front of me and watched, leaning against the counter, his long white sleeves dirty with doing such. "Shame what happened at the mall. That why you out so early?"

I took a long swig of ale and looked at him. "You already hear about that?"

He smiled. "Small Indiana town, word travels fast." He turned around and grabbed himself a bottle and popped the cap same as he did mine with ease. He came over to where I sat and raised his bottle in the air.   "To the afterlife. Wherever we may wind up."

I clinked his glass and watched as he downed half the bottle. I looked off into the distance and stared, remembering the last words Simon the Ghost had said to me. "Your gift can't really help anyone, can it?" I closed my eyes and finished my drink.

"Can I ask you something, Mr. Hunter?" I asked, not making eye contact.

He turned and put his hands on his hips. "I didn't realize I had gone full bartender quite yet, but proceed," he joked.

I swirled my empty bottle around like a pendulum. "Where do you think we go when we die?"

Mr. Hunter actually looked taken aback. He laughed nervously until he saw the seriousness on my face.

"You ask the big questions, don't you, Mr Crane." He turned around and got another bottle out. I reached for my wallet behind me and he gestured to me that it was on the house. "I have been surrounded by books with those answers for years and you know what?" I leaned forward eagerly. "I haven't read a single one." He stood and walked over to his desk and opened up a drawer on the bottom shelf of his desk. He pulled out a very old looking leather bound book from within and walked briskly back over to the bar. He dropped the book in front of me. It was leather bound, with old stained pages, and a lock with a heart kept it closed.

"You know what this is?" he asked seriously.

I looked down at it, afraid to touch it for fear it would break under any amount of pressure. "I'd guess some sort of journal?"

Mr. Hunter swiped it up and held it firmly in his strong hands. I could see the leather bending under his thumb.

"This was my granddaughter's journal," he finally said. "It's all I have left of her. She died young, and she died scared. Murdered by someone that was never caught. And I will never see her again." He leaned forward and eyed me coolly. "And you came into this town years ago, claiming you can speak to the dead."

I felt the need to flee. I had never seen Mr. Hunter this defensive before. This really meant something to him, and I got the feeling he had been wanting to say this for a long time. Maybe the bar had been too busy before?

I looked at him suspiciously. "Mr Hunter, if you are asking me to try to find your granddaughter and speak to her, I am sorry to say it might be tricky…"

He slammed a hand down on the bar and glared. "No Crane, I'm not asking you to find her, I'm asking you to stop…this. This…charade. Even if it were true that you can speak to ghosts, we don't need to know. No one needs to know until it is their time. Do you understand me?"

I opened my mouth to respond but all I could do was blink. Twice today I'd been attacked about my ability, but this one stung. A lot. And if this is the way that one of the nicest men in town thought, then I can only imagine that most of the others in town thought the same. Maybe they were right. Maybe calling me a freak was their nice way of telling me to stop this.

"I asked, do you understand?" Mr. Hunter repeated. He didn't sound mad. He sounded…concerned. Like the first fatherly advice I'd been given in years. I needed some fresh air. Mr. Hunter leaned against the counter, clutching the journal tight. "We only get this one life, Mr. Crane. You're a good man. Stop playing with these citizens' hearts." I turned and walked toward the door. Resisting the urge to cry.

Mr. Hunter sounded vulnerable and sad when he spoke behind me. "I think it's time for you to leave, sir."

"Yeah," I responded, opening the door on my way out into the darkening streets. "It's time for me to go home."

CHAPTER

FIVE

I felt hollow. I don't remember how long I walked for but it had to have been hours. The moon was beginning to show up overhead in the summer sky, and my feet were beginning to hurt. I'd been lost in my own thoughts and looking onto the ground for so long that when I looked up I was startled by my reflection in a darkened shop on the street. I stared at my reflection horrified by what I saw. My eyes looked tired, my skin was pale, and to make matters worse I was still wearing my disgusting uniform. That smug pretzel was on my shoulder mocking me.

I yanked my polo off over my head and flung it on the ground stomping on it viciously. Dirty footprints stained the cheap fabric. My black T-shirt that was underneath was already damp from sweat and I needed to get home. But where was home? I'd walked so far I barely recognized this side of town. Traffic flew by me as I chucked my uniform into a trash can. I looked up at a nearby road sign. I didn't recognize the name. I reached into my pocket and got my cell phone out. I never text or make many calls, being the total social pariah that I am, but it still has its uses.

I tapped the screen to access my GPS app and was met with a black screen. Dead. Who knows the last time I charged it.

"Please turn on," I pleaded to my dead phone. I held it tightly, trying to channel some miraculous energy into it. Hey it works on people…maybe technology?

No…no it doesn't.

I cursed inside my head as I bit down on the phone in anger trying to think. I unclenched my jaw after I heard the start of a crack in the glass. Only I could get lost in a town this small. That's what I get for walking around all the time with my head down. As I began to walk up and down the street, trying to find something, anything that I recognized, I heard a sound that made my heart skip faster than it had since I was a little kid.

Bang.

Crash.

Crunch.

It didn't sound exactly like it had the many times I had closed my eyes and I was pretty damn sure I'd been fully awake when I heard it. I wanted to run. I wanted to escape it however I could.

"Hello?" I heard my own voice say, steadily.

Damn my big mouth.

To my surprise however, there was no response. I waited, and watched but heard and saw nothing. I always heard the saying that curiosity killed the cat. Well I'm not a cat, and curiosity got the better of me and so I decided to investigate.

Sometimes I wish I was a cat. Maybe I wouldn't have been so curious.

I went toward where I heard the sound. Visions of hospitals and orphanages flashed in my mind the last time I came into contact with something like that. It was the most fear

I'd ever felt in my life, and I was feeling overwhelmed as those feelings came flooding back into me.

I found myself near an alleyway close to an apartment building, not too unlike my own. I noticed a dumpster that looked like it had been hit hard, a dent lay on top of the railing. I walked up to it and instinctively kicked it. Bang.

My foot hung in midair. It was an almost identical sound to the one I'd heard moments before. Maybe a little softer, but the sound all the same. I looked around into the night for anything that caught my eye. Anything to help me at all see what made the sound of…

"Sir?"

Crash.

A sound echoed as I found myself falling against the dumpster as a young female voice came from somewhere. I turned around violently, looking.

"Who said that? Show yourself."

A small girl came out from the shadows. She was no more than five or six, and she was dressed in a blue dress. Her eyes were a beautiful shade of a similar color and her hair was matted in a pretty sense, and blonde as a flower. She looked sad, scared, and alone.

And I could see right through her.

I straightened up, backing away slowly. "Little girl, are you…okay? I mean…do you…"

The little girl's eyes began to fill with tears as she looked down at her hands, seeming to notice for the first time that she could see through them too.

"Sir…am I… a…a ghost?"

I took a few more steps back. I hadn't seen a ghost so young before. I'd never been in the presence of one who had lost their life so young. I'd never seen one so innocent lose so much. Then something caught the corner of my eye. I turned and looked down the alley, and there lying on the ground I saw a little girl. Dressed in a blue dress, with eyes that were once a similar color, and matted hair as blonde as a flower, and whose skin was slowly growing paler as the blood poured from the side of her head.

Crunch.

"Yeah," I said in a hushed whisper. "Yeah I think you are."

CHAPTER

SIX

I ran my fingers through my hair and tried to control my breathing. There not two feet away was the body of a little girl. I reached for my phone and held it tightly. I needed to call someone but the phone was dead. My phone was just as dead as this little….gah…

"Sir, are you okay?"

The voice was so tiny and sweet. I turned around and saw the little one coming up to stand next to me.

"Umm...hey, you might not want to see what's over there."

I expected a scream. I expected her to freak out. Even the most hardened cop could be squeamish over a dead body. But instead she looked almost quizzical about it.

"Is that me?"

"Yes. It is. I'm…I'm so sorry. Do you know what…how…"

"I look like I'm sleeping pretty soundly."

I smiled as nicely as I could, choking back tears. "Yeah. You look…shit."

The little girl looked up at me angrily. "You swore."

"Yeah, sorry about that." I looked down at her and nodded, smiling. "Umm, yeah you look peaceful."

"What do you think I'm dreaming about?"

"Ummm…I'm sure it's very nice things." I was stumbling hard. I never spent any time around any kids, let alone ghost ones.

"Do you think I'll wake up soon?"

"Oh fuck me, this is hard," I thought to myself. I couldn't answer. I couldn't think of a single thing to say. I had to get away from this. I had to run. What could I possibly do?

And for a moment I almost did. A part of me thought about running the opposite direction and leaving this girl alone. She was already dead, what's the worst that can happen? She is young and will find her peace somewhere right? She had to.

Then a voice rang in my ears. "Your gift can't help anyone can it?"

My gift. The ability I owned was a curse. Haunted day and night by people I barely knew, seeing and hearing ghostly howls in the night that may or may not be a cry for help. These were lost spirits. Spirits that didn't know a guy like me existed. Spirits that had no one but each other to talk to and all of them lost trying to find a connection to reality again. I could have been this connection for so many and I have squandered years of it away feeling sorry for myself.

The little girl turned and looked at me with saddened eyes. "Sir, do you think you can help me?"

I took a deep breath and looked right back at that little girl. You know when they say when you look into someone's eyes you are looking into the depths of their soul? Well I was looking directly at this little girl and she was nothing but soul.

"Come on," I said to myself more than anyone. "Let's see what this gift can really do."

CHAPTER

SEVEN

I walked up to the little girl as confidently as I could. I crouched down beside her and smiled my most friendly smile. "So, let's see if we can get you some help, huh?"

The little girl sniffled, and looked back at her body. "Yeah, I think that would be a good idea."

I looked down at my dead phone in my hand and pocketed it. "Do you know somewhere where I can make a call?"

She thought for a moment, putting her little fingers on her chin. "My Mommy has a cell phone, but she is sleeping."

"Okay," I said rubbing my hands together. "Do you know where you live?"

She turned around and pointed to the large building beside us. "We live in this big building beside us. Apartment. 516."

The girl was quick. I think it took me till I was ten before I ever even learned the family phone number. "Okay, let's see what we can do. Can you wait right here for me?"

The little girl looked shy for the first time since I'd seen her. "Mommy says I'm not supposed to talk to strangers." I chuckled lightly. She was a good kid.

I held out my hand toward her and smiled. "Well my name is Thomas Crane. Pleased to meet you."

The little girl smiled and reached out to touch my hand, and her face fell into immediate loss as it passed right through me.

Damn it.

How could I forget the most basic rule of being a ghost? I tried my best to hide it.

"So, can you tell me your name?"

She wrinkled her nose, still staring at her hand. "My name is Sophie."

"Well, Sophie. Let's see about getting your corpse…umm…body somewhere safe, yeah?"

"Okay, Thomas," she said matter of factly, as if we had known each other for years. Kids are funny that way.

"That is a very pretty dress, Sophie," I said, trying to ease her pain and confusion.

"Thank you," she said cheerfully. "My mommy made it for me. Blue is my favorite color."

What the hell was I getting myself into?   I was just about to lead her around the building away from the body when a scream echoed through the alley. Sophie covered her ears and closed her eyes as I frantically turned around. The loud scream was then followed by a loud barking followed by additional voices yelling. Then I saw a woman on her cell phone, another holding a dog on a leash and another couple running away from me.

"Yes? Police? I want to call about a murder. Yes, he is still here. He is standing right in front of me! He killed a little girl, damn it!" Rush hour.

I looked down as the blood from the girl slowly surrounded my shoes. Vinny was right…Fuck Me.

CHAPTER

EIGHT

I'll be honest, the following moments after the blue and red lights showed up are a bit of a blur. I don't remember my face hitting the ground as I heard the snap of a pair of cuffs around the wrist; although my jaw sure felt it. I don't remember the car ride to the Southern Indiana police station, where I was booked and fingerprinted and shoved against a wall to have my picture taken. I don't remember being shoved into the interrogation office and chained to a desk as a light was shone brightly in my face. Okay, maybe I remember it all very well, but I sure as hell didn't want to.

I'd never been arrested before. I hardly ever got in trouble let alone handcuffed in front of a little girl. Little girl…Sophie. How was I ever going to find her again? How was I going to make sure she was alright? My thoughts were interrupted as a large file slammed down in front of my face.

"How are you doing tonight, Mr. Crane?…Comfy?"

I jolted up, pulling the handcuffs tight around my wrist. I hadn't even heard him come in.

"Jumpy aren't you?" he continued, pacing the room. "The guilty usually are."

"What are you talking about, Connor?" I questioned. (Like I said, small town, you know everyone…even the police.)

"That's Detective Connor to you, freak," he sharply responded.

Detective Leroy Conners. High school athlete turned good guy turned stone cold bully. He was tall, maybe a few inches above six foot, blonde military hair cut, and lean. If he wore a fedora and trench coat he would look like a sixties noir hero. He went by the book, followed the book, and knew nothing but the book. And I am pretty sure everyone on the police force hated him. He loved it.

"Detective Conner," I said, drawing out the word as annoyingly as I could. "I don't think you are allowed to call your guest a 'freak.' Bad for morale." I winked at him. I was already in trouble for a crime I didn't commit. I figured what the hell.

He slammed his fist down on the table in front of me. "We have five bodies that have been found in the last two weeks, Crane. You know that?"

I thought for a second before responding. "I think I heard something about that on the radio."

He continued to pace the room. "And I just found you at the scene of the crime, talking incoherently to yourself over the body of our youngest victim. She was just a kid. And her blood is all over your shoes."

I looked down under the table. Sure enough, the bottom of my sneakers were caking up with a crimson hue. I almost threw up. It made sense. This cop was an asshole, but it sure did not look good for me in this moment.

"And you think I killed her."

"We KNOW you killed her. You were seen by no less than 6 witnesses."

"I didn't do it. I promise you."

"Sure, right. Then who did?"

"I don't know. I found her like that."

"Really? A likely story…and you didn't call the police because?"

"My phone was dead."

"Didn't bother getting help?"

I felt my hands getting hot. I felt like screaming. I felt like getting angry, but the truth of the matter was, was that this did not look good. I was running out of steam. What happened again? I heard a sound, I found the girl, and I…talked to her ghost? What choice did I have? I was already the freak of the week, I wouldn't dare jeopardize more of my sanity. I had to just buckle down and just…

"I talked to her."

Me and my big mouth.

Conner just stared at me for a long moment and crossed his arms. "You talked to who?"

I looked at him nervously as I muttered "Sophie. The little girl who died is named Sophie."

He ran his fingers through his short blonde hair. "How do you know her name?"

"She told me." I hesitated. "I mean, her ghost told me."

Conner's face turned red with hate. "A little girl died tonight, Crane. A little girl who died by your hand died and you're going to sit here and play games with us?"

I looked down at my wrists, which were slowly growing swollen. I was cooked. And for a crime I didn't commit. You know that instinct I had when I first saw the little girl and I wanted to run? I'm starting to think I should have taken it.

"Mr. Crane. You are under arrest for the murder of a…"

"I can prove it!" I blurted out.

Conner stopped dead in his tracks and eyed me up and down. "Prove what? That the freak finally snapped?"

I tried to stand but the shackles made it a very awkward manuver. "I think I can prove who killed her. Let me go back to the apartment. Let me help."

Conner stared at me, emotionless, and to my surprise responded in a very mild, civil tone.

"Help? How can you possibly help that girl?"

I looked down at the table and closed my eyes. "Because I have to."

I am not sure how long I was in custody, but the sun was slowly coming up over the horizon. I was exhausted. I could feel my eyes growing heavier with every mile of the police cruiser's wheels. My wrists were still pretty sore by the time I was escorted back to the police car. I was no longer cuffed. Granted, as far as the police knew I was telling the truth, aside from the whole speaking to her ghost thing. I really did find her like that and the situation went sideways before I could make the proper move. Running away just wasn't my style.

Conner drove while I sat in the back of the police cruiser. He didn't say anything but I could feel his eyes piercing into my skull like daggers through the rearview mirror. I was fortunate enough that they were giving me this chance at all, but I sure as hell was not out of the woods yet. How was I going to prove anything? I didn't have a plan, and Sophie didn't have time to tell me much about her death. If I was going to stay out of jail tonight, I wasn't just going to need a miracle, I was going to need an angel.

"What the hell is going on over there?" I heard Conner say to himself. I saw him looking out the window at a young woman who was spray painting some amazing graffiti on the side of a brick building. She was wearing a black tank top, arms covered in tattoos, beautiful dark hair and those legs… "Riley?"

Hello angel.

Conner turned the car into a parking lot and got onto his radio. "This is Unit 435, we have a number on 5th. Subject is vandalizing building. I'm gonna go check it out."

"You're clear for entry Unit 435," I heard the radio's static reply.

"Roger." Conner opened the door and stepped out. I watched as he walked away toward Riley, who was hard at work drawing some flames around a very realistic skull. I wiggled in the car seat and tried the door. Locked. Of course. Come on, where is the trust?

I looked around at where we were. I could just make out the corner of the apartment that I was pretty sure I ran into Sophie. It had been dark, but I could see the dislodged dumpster sticking out from behind the alley. I shook my head in disbelief that I was back here. More deadly mental images to add to my collection of nightmares.

I watched as Detective Conner got closer to Riley. She didn't seem to see or hear him. I presumed headphones. Riley always was one for good taste and style. I probably shouldn't have laughed as hard as I did when Detective Conner poked her shoulder and he took a can of paint to the face as she turned around.

Any other person in town would have been terrified of assaulting a cop. Not Riley. Not this girl. She stared at him with a fire in her eyes reserved for those who talk in a theater. She had a passion behind those eyes that made you know she was not one to mess with. I even saw Detective Conner take a step back, wiping the white paint from his eyes. Then the shouting started.

"You can't go sneaking up on a woman like that! Get out of here, Leroy."

"You are vandalizing personal property. Leave now before this gets worse."

"What happened to art being a part of freedom of speech? You think this disgusting wall cares if I add a little life to it?"

I could tell Conner was getting insecure. I mean who couldn't when the goth bombshell of that caliber was angry with you?

"Well the city of…"

"Oh fuck this city," Riley interrupted. She threw her can of paint down and began to storm off down the street. "Fuck this town and fuck you."

I watched, silently cheering from the back seat of the police car. I dared Detective Conners to call her out for littering.

Conners pinched the bridge of his nose and breathed heavily before bending down to pick up the half empty can of spray paint. He looked it over before chucking it into the trashcan on the corner of the street.

"All's clear. Vandalism taken care of. No report made."

"10-4," The radio replied.

Way to go Riley.

Conner watched her walk away before staring back at the building that Riley had been vandalizing. He pulled out a notepad and scribbled something down before heading inside. I breathed heavily. Good, a few more moments to figure out how I was going to get out of this. I had to get to Sophie. I had to get her to find a way to show me how she had died. Only she would have the knowledge that would get me out of this and clear my name. But how? I have always been able to confront ghosts. I have either seen them in passing or they have come to me. Only once had I ever tried to go looking for a ghost on my own but I never found him.

I had tried for many years while I was still in the orphanage to go looking for my father. I had gone down every path I knew and while I knew my chances were slim, I knew he was out there. After so many years though that hope slowly goes away.

This time though, the trail was fresh. I barely knew anything about this little girl but I knew where she was and where she had been. I knew she was scared, and lost, and confused of this new world she was in. Even I wasn't sure how it all worked. I needed answers, and I needed them fast.

Tap tap tap.

I jumped and looked in the direction of the sound. There on the other side of the car's window stood a very confused goth girl. "What the hell are you doing, Thomas?"

"Uhh…" was all I could say. I could feel the embarrassment really seeping in.

"I didn't take you for the 'bad boy,'" she said with a twinkle in her eye.

I couldn't speak. All I could do was laugh like a school boy. There goes the street cred.

"Seriously," she repeated. "What happened?"

I leaned back in the seat and spoke through the window. "The usual freak stuff." She seemed to laugh at that. "Was it a ghost thing?" I nodded.

She reached into her pocket and brandished a small box. She opened and seemed to pick through it very delicately, biting her lip. She soon pulled out a small device that looked like a screwdriver mixed with a swiss army knife but way smaller before she dropped to her knees out of view. I could hear strange noises coming from the outside of the door.

"Riley? What are you doing?" I said nervously.

"What?" she replied. "I came back here to vandalize his car anyways. I figured busting out his newest criminal must make him look real bad."

I couldn't help but be amazed at her fluidity with her lockpick. This clearly wasn't the first time she had busted open a lock. My amusement quickly went away as I considered the repercussions.

"Riley, I appreciate this but I am in a lot of trouble. I don't think running from the police is going to look very good for me right now. And aren't you on really bad terms with them as well?"

She smiled a devilish grin. "The cops can't pin any of this on me. I know how to cover my tracks. And as for you, you should be fine. Besides, what are ghosts best at?"

The door popped open and I was greeted by the warm new morning air. I stretched and gave Riley a thankful glance. "Ghosts are best at not being seen."

NINE

Riley and I took off into the new day sun into a nearby alley. A part of me wished I could see the look on Detective Conner's face when he got back to his cruiser, but I figured it best to let my imagination take over that one. I didn't need to give him the satisfaction of giving him another reason to put me behind bars.

I hid in the shadows with Riley close by and waited, trying to catch my breath. We were about three blocks away from Sophie's apartment. I wanted to get there as fast as I could but if anything Detective Conner would go there first to make sure I wasn't trying to hide any evidence.

Which of course I had nothing to hide, but they didn't know that.

"Come on, Thomas," I told myself. "Pull it together."

"So what's the plan? Why were you under arrest?"

I began to tell Riley about the sound I heard in the alley and about the little girl I'd found. I told the part about interacting with her ghost as timidly as possible. I'm still not fully convinced Riley believes any of it, but she seemed highly engaged the whole time I told her about my situation.

"So let me get this straight. You found the body of a little girl who lost her life for reasons that no one knows, and you spoke to her ghost just long enough for you to become wanted for murder?" Riley asked, leaning against the alley wall.

"Yeah pretty much," I replied.

There was a moment of silence.

"That's pretty mental," she finally said.

I leaned against the opposite side of the alley and stared at my feet. "Yep. I'm the coolest."

Riley seemed to be putting it all in her head a lot better than I had. She began to delicately pace the alley and muttering to herself while giving me the occasional sideways glance. She had a quality about her that made me feel safe and I was very glad she was on my side. I had only known Riley about four or five years but no one had ever listened to me the way she did, and for a brief moment while watching her I had forgotten what sort of danger I was really in. She stopped pacing and put her hands on her hips. "So where did you find the body?"

"Behind a dumpster, about twenty four hours ago," I replied.

She stopped pacing and took off down the alley. She looked up at a ladder that was hanging from a nearby balcony and looked around. She darted over to a trashcan, picked it up and strategically placed it off to the side of the ladder. She walked away, lined up with the wall before making a running leap and jumping onto the trashcan, then vaulting herself up against the wall, jumping off of it and clinging to the ladder. She pulled herself up as if she were a feather and planted her feet on the steel platform above.

"Well, let's get going," she said downward at me.

I had to check that my jaw wasn't on the floor. And to check to make sure that it wasn't too obvious how much that had aroused me.

"Where did you learn that?" I called up to her.

"I don't go home much. I hang out in the streets pretty often. Sometimes I learn a thing or two," she replied snarkily.

I looked at the trashcan, the wall, then the ladder. I lined up my run and started sprinting. This is it. My chance to impress the woman of my dreams. I got this. I got this. I got this.

Trip. Clang. Dang.

I jumped onto the trash can and didn't predict my own weight. The trashcan caved in and fell over with my leg wrapped around it. I vaulted off the wall allright, but not nearly the way I had wanted.

"Ow…" I finally managed to say.

I could hear Riley giggling above me. "One sec."

She disappeared from behind the corner of the building where the steel platform wrapped around the building. She was only gone for about two minutes before she came back around with a garden hose tied to something I couldn't see. She threw it over the side of the railing and secured it, motioning for me to grab onto it.

I looked at the garden hose. My athletic ability had never been one I was particularly proud of. I struggled climbing the rope in gym class. I could already see myself making a fool of myself all over again. I wrapped my bony fingers around the green rubber of the hose and pulled. It was secure. I looked up its long thin body, vertigo finally setting in. I craned my neck all the way up until I saw Riley looking down at me, that sly grin across her lips. I had to do this. For Riley, for myself, and for Sophie.

"So are you gonna climb it or what?"

The voice rattled my ears. It startled me greatly, not because of the voice per say but from where it came from. Suddenly, I heard it again. "Thomas, climb it! You can do it."

I looked down and there was that little girl. Smiling brightly ear to ear, her blonde hair curling over her shoulders with an aura of brightness all around her.

"Sophie?" I proclaimed my own excitement matching hers.

"Oh no you don't," I heard Riley say above me. "Don't you go using your 'ghost' ability to get out of climbing up this thing."

"No," I defended. "It's Sophie! She is…she's here!"

"Hello," Sophie said delightfully, looking up at Riley. Riley obviously didn't see nor hear her.

"Hello!" Sophie said again, more intensely. She was clearly getting agitated.

"Hey, Sophie. Riley can't hear you. But I'm here. I promise you, I'm here. And we are here to help you."

Sophie's eyes never left Riley. She was looking at her flustered and annoyed. "Why won't she say "Hi"? It's very rude of her."

I looked up at Riley. "Yeah she can be intimidating. But she is the most loyal friend anyone could ask for."

Riley rolled her eyes and grabbed onto the hose. She swung her legs over the railing and slid down it like some sort of superhero, effortlessly. "If this is your way to try to impress me, you're doing a shit job." She crossed her arms, waiting for an explanation.

I looked at Riley and then at Sophie. "Hey Sophie, this is Riley Blake. She is going to help us figure out how you died."

Riley looked at me with a questionable glance before turning her head to look at where I was addressing Sophie. She unfolded her arms and for a brief moment, I thought she was going to extend her hand to her. I almost told her that it wouldn't do any good, but I figured I would wait. Maybe Sohie could do something, anything, to shed some truth on what I'd been telling her for the past few years.

Riley took a step forward and then turned her head to me. "We don't have time for this.

We gotta clear your name. Come on."

She turned and grabbed the garden hose, beginning to rapidly shimmy up it. I looked at Sophie who was looking at her shoes, twiddling her fingers.

"She can't see me?"

I looked back at Riley. "No, she can't. As new as this world is to you, it is to her too." I turned to Sophie. "She will come around."

I heard Riley huff and mumble something as she got to the top of the steel platform.

"She is very pretty," Sophie finally said.

"Yeah. She's a knock out," I agreed.

"Are you going to keep staring at me or are you going to get your ass up here?" Riley spun around, frustrated.

I wanted to keep staring, admittedly, but I got to my feet and headed over. This time I grabbed the hose and started to pull myself up. I looked down and I saw Sophie trying to help me, but her hands kept fading through my legs. She still had a look of determination, I didn't dare tell her it wasn't helping. Somehow it did give me the motivation to inch my way up. Not as fast as Riley, but I reached the top out of breath, but proud of myself.

"Guess you aren't all skin and bones, huh?" Riley said.

"I work better under pressure," I panted, lying on my back.

Below me, I could hear Sophie cheering and clapping her hands in excitement. Riley extended her hand and helped me to my feet. I looked down and saw Sophie giving me a thumbs up from below, before disappearing in a cloud of mist, and then reappearing a few feet away at the other end of the alley. I guess sometimes being a ghost just comes naturally to some.

Riley and I got to the other end of the platform and she helped me get down to the ground. There was a series of slips and tumbles but I managed to land safely on the ground, despite my legs shaking from the fall. Riley on the other hand, well, she managed to make it look easy. She waved me over to the edge of the alley wall, and raised her hand to silence me.

"Look over there. Cops."

I looked. Sure enough, there were two cop cars and a few officers wandering around the apartment where Sophie had died. One of them was of course Detective Leroy Conner. He did not look happy. It didn't help that he still had a smear of white paint under his chin.

"What the hell were you thinking, Conner?" an officer asked.

"Yeah, guess they will promote any old smuck to Detective these days huh?" said another.

Conner reached into his pocket and pulled out a cigarette. He went to light it but his lighter kept sparking. He aggressively put it back in his pocket. I could see Riley smiling at his misfortune from my peripheral.

"Come on, guys." Conner said, anguished. "He escaped. Could have happened to anyone."

The first cop scoffed. "True, but it happened to you. The mighty Leroy Conner." Both cops began to laugh aggressively. I almost felt bad for him. Almost.

"Need I remind you of the Hudson case, boys? Remember how the two of you let three convicts go when you turned your backs? And how I helped cover up for you?" The two cops silenced up.

"So when I say, he escaped under the mighty Leroy Conner…" He drew out his own name, defiantly…"I mean it when I say that this guy means business. Now find him." Shit. When Conner wants things done, he knows how to bark orders.

The two cops walked away like two dogs with their tails between their legs and pretended to look at the ground in search of clues. Conner did that thing I saw him do before when he pinched the bridge of his nose in annoyance. He looked up for a split second and then his head snapped in our direction.

The wind got knocked out of me as Riley shoved me back into the shadows. "Hush," she demanded. I could hear Conner's heavy footsteps getting closer and closer. I bit my lip, ready to be hauled out of the darkness and hauled out into the sun.

Suddenly, I heard a car door slam. Lights turned on from the nearby swat car and it peeled off into the street. "Hey, stop that car!" I heard from one of the cops.

I peered my head out from behind the wall and saw the two cops and Conner chasing after a police car. One of the cops started to get into the driver's seat before Conner grabbed his shoulder and pulled him aside, jumping into his place behind the wheel. The other two climbed into the vehicle and sped off after the car. It wasn't long before the sounds of the sirens dropped down over the hill.

I looked at Riley whose eyes were wide and her mouth was open in shock and joy. We exchanged glances before I turned away from her. "You don't see that every day, do you Sophie?"

Silence.

"Sophie?" I looked around. She had disappeared. Had that little girl...stolen the police car? Impossible. Vinny had told me it takes months, sometimes years for a ghost to master the ability to manipulate objects. Sophie had been a ghost for less than a day. How did she already have that type of talent?

"Now is our chance. We gotta get inside that apartment and find out what is going on," Riley said, excitedly.

"But..." I was still glancing around trying to find Sophie. "We can't just go sneaking around the apartment. We don't even know what we are looking for."

Riley was already running around the corner and heading for the stairs of the building. "Don't you watch detective shows? If you want to clear your name, you return to the scene of the crime."

I followed her. "But she died in the alley. Her body was over there," I said pointing toward the askew dumpster, desperately hoping for any excuse to not go snooping in someone else's house.

"Didn't you tell me her ghost said she lived here?" she replied. The way she said ghost gave me a hint she still didn't believe me.

"Yeah."

She shrugged. "Well, the cops have already cleaned up that mess. Now we go to the source. Where she was before the death. Come on, you said you wanted answers." I sighed and followed her up the steps. I was just racking up the criminal charges. May as well go for a record.

The door to the main hallway of the apartment was unlocked. Down it there were twelve doors, each leading to a room housing a small apartment.

"So, what room are we looking for?" Riley asked uncertainly.

"Sophie told me it was room number 516."

Riley didn't make eye contact. "And you didn't just pull that number out of your ass?" I closed my eyes. Damn it. I thought Riley had been the one who understood. Now she was just falling into place with all the others.

We reached the end of the hallway. To the right there was a staircase that led up to the upper floors. Riley grabbed the railing and began to climb.

"You don't have to do this, you know," I said, looking guilty.

"Do what?" she replied, still climbing.

"You don't have to pretend to be my friend. I know what I'm like. I know what the town thinks, and you can stop pretending."

Riley stopped on the steps. She didn't turn around but I could see her shoulders tense up. "You want to know what I am here?" I didn't respond. "I'm here because you're different. Everyone always treats me like some sort of object. But not you. You have always seen me for me."

Zing, snap. I could feel an arrow pierce my heart. I was always kind to Riley, but I certainly wanted to be more than friends. She was the ideal goth girlfriend, anyone would be lucky to have her. Suddenly I was flooded with guilt.

"And, you're really weird. I like that in my friends," she continued.

Butterflies. If I could have levitated off the ground and floated to the ceiling like some sixties cartoon in that moment I would have.

I took a step toward the stairs. "So…you believe me when I say I can speak to ghosts?"

She took a few more stairs up. "I want to…" she whispered.

CHAPTER
TEN

WE approached room 516 with care. It looked like any other door in the building. Old wood, very grainy, with a sloppy white paint job over it. Yet, something about it felt off. Almost offputting. I suppose it could be that just over a day ago a little girl had lost her life outside, or the fact that we were about to go into a stranger's house, or maybe it was the fact that Riley was already pulling out her lockpicking kit with eagerness.

"Riley? Stop that, we don't even know what we are doing yet."

"You want inside don't you?" she replied in a harsh whisper.

"No. No I don't. I am in enough trouble as it is and I don't think that…"

"Then what the hell are we doing here? I thought you wanted to clear your name?"

"I do! But I don't think breaking and entering is the best way to go about doing that."

"Then why did we come all this way together if you aren't going to grow some balls and clear it?"

"Because I can't do this alone!" I said, much louder than I intended.

Before Riley could reply, we were interrupted by the shaking of a door handle as the door to apartment 516 rattled violently before slowly opening with a haunting creak that made Riley and I freeze in place. The door opened slowly, softly, but with the delicate ease of a loose hinge. We braced ourselves, ready to be greeted, shouted at, or shot. Who knows what was on the other side of that door.

No one.

Riley and I looked at each other and then at the empty, open doorway. No one there. I at least expected to see a ghost or something. I even blinked a few times to make sure that there really wasn't anyone there. Nothing. Riley took a step forward and looked around the apartment.

"Riley, we can't," I whispered under my breath.

"Come on, I don't think anyone is home." She walked in a crouch, her black skirt flowing with every step.

I followed her in, afraid to be alone in that hallway. I looked around the apartment, it was a nice place. Big living room with a connecting kitchen, a hallway leading down with two doors on one side and one on the other. I could just make out some paper lettering that read Sophie's Room in the center of the lonely door. I made my way to the hallway and admired it. This apartment was three times the size of mine and five times as homely. I leaned against the door imagining my life in such a place before I heard something smash behind me.

"Damn it," Riley began to curse.

I looked at the broken dish that had fallen off the kitchen table and smashed on the wooden floor. "That's okay, we weren't trying to stay inconspicuous anyways." I rolled my eyes as Riley desperately started looking for a broom.

"Shut up and help me clean this up," Riley hissed.

I began to move toward her when a quiet voice came from the hallway. It started as a hum, but then it started to sing. It was a children's nursery rhyme that I remember hearing from my mother when I was just a child. I looked down the wall and started to tiptoe toward the sound. It was growing louder and louder. Sophie's room. I reached for the doorknob and turned the handle to look inside. I suddenly felt a gush of cold air and a gasp of a female woman. The door slammed shut, nearly jamming my fingers. I looked at the door in shock. I'd never felt such a ghostly force before. I'd never felt that sort of power. "Sophie?"

I gathered my courage and pushed the door open. I stared in wonder as a wooden rocking chair continued to rock, its creaking wood muttering every sway. I quickly looked around the room but there was no one there. An open window made the light weight curtains sway in the morning breeze. "Sophie?" I repeated.

Silence.

The room felt cold. I almost felt like I was being watched. The rocking chair was swaying slower now, and at the foot of it lay a children's book. I'd seen it before. Goodnight Misty the Cat. It was a children's book that had been made into a song at some point. The song I had heard someone singing just moments ago.

I am no singer, but I tried to hum what I remembered of it from childhood.

Goodnight moon
Watch over my home
Till morning we roll out the mat

Goodnight my friends
Goodnight those within
From Misty the Cat

I waited a while for an answer, or for someone to continue the song, but I was met with silence.

Bleak, cold silence. The rocking chair coming to a stop made me bow my head, somehow feeling a sense of calm in the room. I was interrupted from my peace as Riley stomped down the hallway next to me, holding a cloth around her finger. "And you were worried about me making noise? Quit slamming doors," She retorted.

I didn't argue. Instead I followed her down the hall. "You okay?"

She looked into a room on the wall, and went inside. As the light flipped on I saw it was the family bathroom. She flipped the water faucet on and began running her hand under the water. "Damn glass cut my hand." She vigorously began dabbing at her hand with a wet cloth.

I leaned against the door, contemplating my thoughts. "Maybe I should just turn myself in."

Riley flipped her hand over and started washing the other side. I could tell she was using very warm water. She didn't look up. "Maybe you should."

I looked at her, surprised by her answer. I found my jaw hanging open.

"Or maybe..." she continued. "You can tell me what the hell is going on with you." I stared at her as steam began to fill the bathroom.

"Why do you do this? What is wrong with you that you have to make up these stupid rumors about yourself that you can talk to ghosts? Is it really so hard for you to make friends?"

I stood straight. "I CAN talk to ghosts. I thought of all the people you would believe me."

She threw the cloth down at the sink. "Damn it, Thomas. You're a good guy. You don't need to make shit up to win people over. You think I hang out with you because you think you can talk to ghosts? No. I hang out with you because you are different, weird, and creative, but this? This has got to stop."

Her words echoed very closely to what Mr. Hunter had said. "I can't change who I am, Riley. You think I want this? To be haunted by these visions and sounds daily?" I heard something in the other room make a noise, but I was too upset and defensive to notice it.

Riley turned toward me. "When are you going to grow up, Thomas? This is crazy! You got yourself into this legal trouble and I am trying to help you, a friend, get out of it. But if you can't be honest with me then I don't know what else to do. YOU CAN'T SPEAK TO…"

Just then, there was a squeaking sound coming from the mirror. The condensation from the warm faucet water had made the mirror become cloudy. We both turned to look at the fading reflection as a tiny fingerprint began to spell out HI…RILEY…followed by a tiny happy face.

Riley's face became flushed and white as snow. "Ghost…" she breathed.

I leaned up against the sink, my heart beating fast. "Riley? I'd like you to meet Sophie."

CHAPTER

ELEVEN

I hadn't noticed Riley had gripped my arm, her nails digging into my skin. To her credit, she didn't scream. Didn't even flinch. She just stared at her name written in the mirror. She turned her head and spoke to me, her eyes never leaving the writing. "What is this?"

I put my hand on hers and relaxed her grip. "Sometimes they like to communicate this way. It is almost impossible for a ghost to speak directly to a live being, you know unless they have a…"

"…A near death experience," Riley finished.

I nodded. I had told her of my past. We had spoken at great lengths of our childhoods over many breaks at the mall. I had told her all about how since I lost my dad in the accident, and how I had tried finding my mother to no avail. I think she took my 'being able to speak to ghost' as a coping mechanism. And maybe in its own way it was. And right here and now, the one person I had trusted everything in was finally going to see that I was not a fraud.

"How are you doing this? Is this some sort of trick?" Well damn, maybe not.

"No," I assured her. "This is real, I promise you. Ghosts exist, and one is trying to talk to you right now."

Suddenly the mirror started to make more shapes as a heart was slowly drawn around the face of Riley's reflection.

"If this is your twisted, fucked up way to flirt with me, I gotta say it's unique."

I shook my head. "Trust me, I'm not that clever."

Sophie spoke, "Tell her I think she is pretty."

I grimaced. "Umm…She thinks you are very pretty."

Riley cocked an eyebrow at me. "You sure you aren't trying to flirt with me?" Sophie started jumping up and down, clapping her hands again.

"Can I…can I speak to her?" Riley asked, looking around the bathroom.

I looked at Sophie acknowledging her presence. "She will hear you, but I don't think you will be able to hear her."

Riley nodded and crouched down below the sink. She looked at me nervously, before looking back down. She didn't quite make eye contact with Sophie. Sophie giggled before moving to face her a bit better.

Riley cupped her mouth and whispered, "He isn't so bad either."

My eyes grew wide. I wasn't sure exactly what I heard if I'd even heard right at all. Sophie clapped her hands again and climbed on top of the sink. Her writing and heart were slowly erased and replaced with a giant heart being drawn around both of our reflections.

I looked at Riley nervously, and to my surprise Riley had a giant smile on her face. She turned her beautiful face, her heavy eyeliner piercing back at me and took my hand. All I could do was bite my lip in nervousness. She leaned in and I swear her lips were forming a kiss. She got closer and closer…and…

"You want to come see my room?" Sophie shouted.

I let go of Riley. "Great timing Soph…"

Riley laughed. "What is it?"

I looked down at Sophie. "Sophie wants to show us her room," I said through gritted teeth. "Sophie, the adults are talking."

Riley crouched down again. "Come now Thomas, not in front of the…child?" she asked looking up.

I nodded. Sophie stuck her tongue out at me and tried to grab Riley's hand, but it passed through. Riley still seemed to go with it and followed her out of the bathroom and into the hall. I rolled my eyes, but it was hidden by a huge smile. I'd been surrounded by ghosts all my life. I'd never really been without one to talk to. But for the first time in as long as I could remember I finally didn't feel alone.

The three of us went into the small room with Sophie's name on the door. The rocking chair was still and the book was lying flat. The room was silent and there was not a chill nor sound in the air. I looked at the curtains. They fell among the window sill, completely still. I walked over to it and put my hand near the open window. There was not even a hint of a breeze. I looked out the window and looked down, expecting to see the dumpster below where the girl had died, but it was not at this window.

Riley began wandering the room, looking at the toys on the floor and the pictures on the dresser. She stopped at a photo of a happy couple holding a little girl while standing on a fishing boat. The bottom of the frame read The Brownstone's.

"This your parents?" Riley asked Sopie, not looking anywhere in particular.

"Yes," said Sophie. "That's my mommy and daddy. We were out on the lake fishing." Sophie looked at Riley, and then sadly looked at me in desperation, sadness filling her eyes.

"Yeah," I replied, finally. "Sophie said that was them."

"Tell her about the fish!" Sophie shouted. "Tell her I caught the biggest one!"

I looked down at her and smiled. "It's not nice to brag, Sophie." I started looking around the room myself, trying to figure out where that humming or singing had come from. I started to pick up her toys and squeeze them and gently nudge them just trying to see what had played that familiar music. And what about the scream? And the force that had slammed the door?

Sophie crossed her arms and pouted. I think she tried kicking me a time or two, as well. Thankfully she was too new to the whole ghost experience to become an angry ghost. Nobody likes a howling spectre.

Riley picked up the photo and smiled at it. "Sophie, do you know where your parents are?"

Sophie stopped pouting and ran over to Riley. "Mommy is sleeping. I haven't seen her in a while. Daddy goes out a lot. He usually comes home late angry." Sophie paused and looked back at me. "Daddy scares me sometimes."

I looked up at Riley who was still smiling at the picture. There was a joy in her eyes that I dared not shatter, but she was here to help and I needed to be honest. "Sophie, where is your mommy sleeping?" I choked.

Sophie went to a nearby window and pointed outside. I swallowed hard and wandered over to the window, following her gaze. There on the horizon up on a hill stood a large open field, hundreds of tiny stones surrounded the area in perfect rows.

"Raven's Roost Cemetary," I managed to say.

"Hmm?" Riley asked from across the room.

Sophie nodded. "She went over there and never returned. I think people go there when they want to sleep for a long time."

Damn it… I thought to myself. Sophie's story is so sad. I wondered why she was denied such knowledge at her age. Yeah, she is a young girl but I was fairly certain I had been taught the lessons of death by her age. I had been in my car accident when I wasn't much older than her. Why was she so blinded by the facts of death? And worse yet, how was someone like me going to teach her?

Riley came up behind us, still holding the picture. She looked out the window and nearly dropped the photo. "Sophie, are your parents dead?"

I shot Riley an exasperated look. You can't just drop that on someone this impressionable who doesn't understand that fabric of life and…

"I think my mother is…" Sophie proclaimed.

Oh. Well, maybe this little girl was smarter than I gave her credit for. Riley crouched down and whispered, surprisingly close to Sophie's ear despite not seeing her. "We will take care of you. You're not alone."

Sophie turned around and hugged Riley. Actually HUGGED her. I could see the fabric of Riley's skirt sway in a gust of wind and I could see Sophie's arms actually tighten around her legs. Riley shivered and folded her arms, fighting the urge to chatter her teeth. I looked at her shocked and amazed while Sophie gave me a look of absolute delight.

"Riley…I think she is actually hugging you."

Riley suddenly stopped shivering, and smiled down at her legs. "Thank you, Sophie. You are a very special girl, you know that?"

I stand corrected…this girl is much smarter than I gave her credit for.

TWELVE

HUNDREDS of thoughts were going through my mind. How did she die? Was it a murder? Where was her father in all of this? Who was the person who had been in Sophie's room? Had it been her mother? And if so, why hadn't she wanted to speak to me about her daughter? How did Sophie get here in the first place…?

"Wait…" I paused, my train of thought suddenly derailing. "How DID you get here, Sophie?"

Sophie looked up and beamed. "Thomas, you won't believe it! I drove a car!"   I looked down and felt my eyes close, much like a disappointed father.

"You stole the police car outside?"

"She WHAT?" shouted Riley, smiling bright.

"Yeah!" Sophie said. "I saw you two were in trouble in the alley, so I snuck into one of the police cars and drove away."

I looked at her with amazement. "Wait, did they leave the keys in the car?"

Sophie looked annoyed. "You don't need keys, silly. You just touch the wheel and there you go."

I was about to argue but then I remembered something I'd read about in Mr. Hunters bookstore. If you have a goal in mind in the spirit world, you can possess certain items, or in this case vehicles, to your will. Holy hell, Sophie was one very fast evolving ghost.

"So you possessed a car and drove away?" I asked.

Sophie shrugged.

"That's badass," Riley proclaimed, standing next to me.

I shook my head. "No, you don't understand. She shouldn't be able to do that. Not yet. Especially not at her age."

Riley knelt down and held her hand out to thin air. "Well, you know what they say about girls maturing faster than boys."

Sophie ran up to Riley and gave her a high five. Her hand phased through, but Sophie didn't seem to mind. Riley looked up at me to see if Sophie got the reference. I nodded and turned away.

"Sophie, what do you remember about the day you died?"

Sophie beckoned us to follow and the three of us ran into the hallway. She went up to the last door in the hall and stopped. She looked at us with sad eyes and walked through the door. I went up to it and tried the handle. It was unlocked. I opened the door slowly and steadily. The lights were on, or rather a light. A single bulb hung from the ceiling on a string sitting perfectly still. I looked around the room. There was a single bed with ruffled blankets, a small chair in the corner that looked like it had been reserved for reading, a few empty bottles of various liquors were strewn around the floor, and in the back of the room there was a window with smashed glass that littered the window frame. I took one step inside and I heard a howling wail fill the air, my skin felt like ice. I looked over at Riley who had covered her bare arms tightly around herself, closing her eyes tightly. There was a ting, and a crunch, and then the single light went out. We stood there in silence afraid to take another step.

"What the hell was that?" I asked into the darkness. I felt Riley's arm touch my shoulder as she wandered through the dark. I heard her kick a couple of the bottles on the ground before I heard the click of the lightbulb string. The light came back on and I could see Riley standing in the middle of the room, blinking to regain her sight. She turned around and a look of horror crossed over her face as she looked in my direction.

"Thomas…look," she said, her eyes wide.

I took a step into the room and my shock matched hers as I saw the shards of glass that had been on the windowsill were now knifed into the wall. The doorframe had been pelted with glass, as had the wall behind where we had been standing. I took a few steps back and found myself clinging to Riley tightly.

Riley grabbed my hand and removed it from her hip. "I don't think someone wants us to be here." I nodded slowly and stepped away from her. "Sophie?" I asked grudgingly. "What the fuck was that?"

She stood in front of me and wagged her finger at me. "You swore again."

I started to check myself for cuts or scratches from the glass. "Yeah well, when my life is in fucking danger, I tend to fucking do that."

Sophie seemed to ignore me and wandered over to where the glass had been. "Here is the last place I remember being before everything went kinda fuzzy."

Riley was looking at my face, noticing the sincere concern upon it. "How much danger are you in, Thomas?"

I ran my fingers through my shaggy hair. "This is all a first for me. I've never had the dead try to make me one of them."

Which was true. I'd never really gone out of my way to ever help a spirit, but I had never been outright attacked by one. Sure, my roommate Vinny would play tricks but he never tried to outright harm me. This spirit was vengeful and didn't want us here. I'd been to haunted houses before but this was on another level.

I trudged over to the windowsill, dragging my feet with every step. I put my hands on the sill, mindful of some leftover glass and peered over the edge. Five levels down from where I stood there was the dislodged dumpster, and a dull stained scrap of gravel right next to it. The final resting place of a once cheerful little blonde girl.

"What do you remember?" I asked, still looking down at the road below.

Sophie didn't answer right away. Instead she went over to the bed and knelt down and reached under the bed. She started getting a look of frustration on her face, so I knelt down beside her. I looked under the bed and I saw a tiny felt object. I reached under and I touched it. It was very soft to the touch. I pulled my arm back and revealed in my hand a large book. It was draped in fine leather, but it didn't appear to be very old. It had a strange symbol on the cover and the spine read Passed Relations. I opened the book and flipped through it. There were dozens of incarnations that I had never heard of before. I'd read my fair share of occult history but this was beyond me. This wasn't Ectomancy…this was Necromancy. I stared back at Sophie with a look of horror as she continued to speak.

"I was playing in here. Daddy never liked it when I played in here, but I did. I found this old book and I wanted daddy to read it to me. He got angry and I remember it got really dark, and the next thing I knew I was falling."

"Sophie, did you fall out of the window while you were playing?" I asked.

Riley stepped forward and put a hand on my shoulder. "Even if she fell there is no way there would be this shattered glass if she just fell. Something was thrown through it."

I began rubbing the back of my neck as my thoughts began to wander. If this were true, Sophie's father was an absolute monster who needed to be put behind bars. But what of the shrieking spirit in the bedroom? I couldn't rule out that that hadn't caused it either. And what about me? I knew I wasn't at fault but I had been at the scene of the crime. I had been the first one in for questioning. I was an escaped convict as well as standing in the victim's house. I was most definitely subject one, most wanted numero uno.

"So what do you make of the book?" Riley asked, noticing my expression.

"I don't make much of anything of it yet, but if I know anything it's not good."

Riley looked uncertain. "Can you read it? Will it give Sophie the answers she seeks?"

I skimmed the pages trying to make any heads or tails of it but this was far beyond me. I closed the book and checked the front cover. It read Publication: The Open Page. Courtesy of Edward Hunter.

Son of a bitch.

I looked over at Sophie who was sitting crosslegged on the floor watching me with acute awareness. "No. No, I can't read it. But I think I know who can."

Thump!

Riley heard it before anyone else. She darted for the bedroom door and slammed it shut before locking it from the inside. She had a look of determined frustration when you could hear the sound of a heavy car door slam from outside. I gave both of them a nervous look and then Riley said the most horrifying words I'd heard that day. "The police are here."

Oh fuck.

There was the click of a door and the click of what I can only assume to be a firearm as multiple footsteps could be heard along the tiled ground of the first floor. I could hear distant chattering and orders being given. One of the voices sounded very familiar.

"Right away, Mr Conner." The name made my skin crawl. I could hear the footsteps getting louder and louder as they began to climb the stairs, my heartbeat matching each step.

"What is our next move, Riley?"

Riley bit her lip and looked around. She looked around before frantically running to the bed. "Quick, help me gather up these bed sheets."

I looked at her, my brow cocked. "I don't think now is the best time for a blanket fort."

She rolled her eyes. "Haven't you ever seen a movie…ever? We are going to go out the window." She began tying the sheets to the bed's leg.

"What are you crazy? We can't go out the window!" I looked at her in disbelief.

"You want to go back to the iron house?" She threw the other end of the blanket out the window. I looked to see how far it had gone, it only seemed to cover two floors.

"It's not long enough," I said. "We are gonna have to try something else." The footsteps out in the hallway were getting louder and louder.

"Hey, room 516 is open," I heard a voice say.

Riley looked at me shocked and hissed. "You didn't close the damn door?"

"Well, I thought we would be out of here by now," I snarkled back.

Riley jumped onto the windowsill like some sort of pirate and grabbed the sheet. "We are gonna have to jump."

"Jump?" My heartbeat was going faster.

Bang!

The sound of someone banging on the door grew louder and louder.

"Yeah. We will shoot for the dumpster," she said over her shoulder. I gulped and grabbed onto the sheet.

Crash!

The door gave way and the sound of footsteps swarmed the room.

She jumped out the window placing her feet against the brick of the building as she began to shimmy down. "Hey!" she shouted up. I looked down at her. "You remember our deal right?" I blinked down at her.

"If I die, don't let me stay stuck in this world."

I looked down at her as I got into position. I remembered it well. "I won't let you," I agreed. "I promise."

We jumped for the dumpster.

Crunch!

The feeling of my shock washed over me as I heard the sound of shouting high above me and my limbs being tugged hard by someone's hand. I blinked and the first thing I saw was an angel in black hovering inches from my face yelling "Get up!"

I sat up, my back aching. "We can't stop now, here they come!" shouted Riley. I looked up and saw a very pissed off Detective Conner staring down at me. Despite being a tiny figure above I could tell his eyes were red with anger. He turned around, his coat disappearing around the corner. I could picture him sprinting full force down the stairs finally ready to nab me. I was going back in the slammer unless I got my ass in gear now. I stood up and then remembered the book. I checked under a few of the old cardboard boxes and found its leatherbound evil still intact. Perfect.

Hopping out of the dumpster, my bones had only been saved by a few old boxes and, I hope, what isn't three day old lasagna. I wiped at my clothes as Riley pulled me out. We hit the ground running and we made our way down the street as fast as we could until we couldn't hear the police shouting anymore. She grabbed my arm and we ducked behind a car that was parked on the side of the road. Laying against the wheel, we were both finally able to catch our breath. Here I was on the brink of having my life taken away from me and the one who nearly took it is that one that I care the most about.

"You alive over there, cowboy?" Riley asked, clutching her stomach. She had a nice cut on her arm from the fall.

I patted her leg. "Told you I wasn't gonna let you leave without me."

She grinned. It seemed to cause her pain. "Yeah. Lucky me."

I looked around cautiously seeing if the police were anywhere nearby. We seemed to be in the clear. "We need to get to The Open Page, pronto," I said.

Riley closed her eyes and sighed. "Why would you want to go to that shithole? The guy doesn't even know what he is talking about half the time."

I held the book tightly. "I think he will know about this. We need to get back to my apartment and get to my car. It will be the easiest way to get there."

Riley gave me a suspicious look. "We can't take your car. The police will be all over it." Riley was right. My entire apartment was probably on lockdown.

Riley rose to her feet. "Where is Sophie at anyways?"

As if on cue the car we were leaning against vroomed to life. We both jumped up and took several steps back startled by the sudden engine turning on. I looked in the driver's seat, and for a split second, no one was there. Then Sophie materialized in the seat smiling and honking the horn.

"Look Thomas! I pothessed another car!" her mispronunciation was muttered through the engine.

"Sophie, stop it! We are trying to stay inconspicuous," I whispered through the car window.

Riley smiled. "I gotta admit, I like her style."

I looked at the light blue car and all its horsepower. I don't know much about cars, but I could tell this one was fast. "This will do. Let's get to that bookstore," I said gathering up my strength.

"I'll drive!" the little girl said proudly.

"No!" I said, surprising Riley with my suddenness.

I drove the blue sports car down the road obeying the speed limit, as hard as it was not to speed in this thing, trying to avoid suspicion. Sophie sat in the back still pouting that she wasn't allowed to drive, while Riley sat beside me in the passenger seat, her feet up on the dash. I couldn't help but stare at her occasionally as we drove, but my admiration for her felt different this time.

This didn't look like the same Riley who I had oogled over for nearly five years at the mall. This was a Riley who had seen things. Her eyes weren't fixed in a bored nonchallant stare…they were darting around at every little thing like she was seeing the world for the first time. She wasn't sitting relaxed, she was fidgeting in her seat like she couldn't wait to get out of the car. This was a hardened Riley who had been introduced to the supernatural world and who, honestly, was handling it like an absolute pro. She was a badass and despite finding out that ghosts are real and that there are things in the shadows that maybe you SHOULD be afraid of, she wasn't. She showed no signs of fear. She was somehow more beautiful to me in that very moment than I'd ever seen her before.

I think she felt my eyes on her because she seemed to adjust herself by turning away from me. "You okay, Riley?"

She didn't say anything, but I could see her eyes in the reflection of the window. She looked tired. Hell, it had been some time since either of us had gotten any sleep and she had saved my life on more than one account. Running from the law, it's exhausting.

I pulled the car into a nearby parking garage and went up to the second level. Riley began to look around confused.

"I thought we were going to the bookstore," she said through a hidden yawn.

I stretched. "We are, but we aren't going to be much help to Sophie back there if we are falling asleep standing. I think we should get some rest."

Riley looked in the backseat. To her it was just an empty backseat, but I could see her smile. "What is she like?"

I looked in the rearview mirror and saw Sophie looking back at me, beaming that Riley was taking such an interest.

I leaned back. "She is small and she has pretty blonde hair. She is a bit of a brat." Sophie stuck her tongue out at me. "But she is also caring, curious, and very brave." I turned around and gave her a wink. "We are going to bring you peace, Sophie."

I turned to look at Riley, and she was looking back at me with the gentlest smile across her lips.

"You're a hero to her, you know that, right?"

I looked down at the steering wheel. I didn't feel like a hero, I felt like a burden. I felt like I had overcomplicated so many lives, alive or dead. Riley saw my face and put her hand on mine.

"You have a stronger heart than anyone I know, and I am very glad to be a part of this journey. There is no one I'd rather risk staying stuck in this world with than you."

I turned to respond, but Riley had laid her head on my shoulder and was breathing very soundly. I looked down at her hand in mine and closed my eyes. If I died in my sleep tonight, at least I would die happy.

Sunlight shone through the garage making shadows dance along the concrete pillars. Light bounced off a few other cars, reflecting back into my eyes. I shielded my face and sat up in the car. Riley was leaning against the wall overlooking a small part of the town. I opened the car door and felt my body pop and creak as I straightened up. I hadn't slept that long in a long time. I touched my shoulder where Riley had laid her head. I was going to remember that moment for years to come.

I popped my shoulder and strolled over to where Riley was standing, leaning beside her.

"Morning."

"Morning to you," Riley replied. She still looked tired, but there was a new spark in her eye. After a moment she spoke. "Thank you, by the way. For last night. Keeping me, us, safe. Thank you for caring."

I gave her a sideways hug, feeling her warmth against my side. "There are not many people who would go on this crazy ride with me. You want to get some breakfast?"

Riley moved away from the hug and started heading back to the car. "No, we should get moving. We don't want to be out too late in the morning. The cops will be more mobile."

There was a coldness to her speech. I couldn't quite place it, but it felt unstable. Was it something I said?

I followed her back to the car and got into the driver's seat. Riley was already buckling her seatbelt and staring straight ahead.

"Hey Riley? Are you okay?"

"Yes, Thomas. I'm fine. Let's just go."

I watched her for a second. "You know you can talk to me, right?"

She turned and stared into my eyes for a long time. "I don't…I don't let a lot of people get close, okay? I don't feel safe with most people. So yesterday, when I fell asleep against your arm I felt calm. I…I liked it, okay? And it…scared me." Holy shit.

Maybe she wasn't as brave and confident as I thought. I mean, she is the strongest woman I know, and she is openly admitting that she feels safe and calm with me? I didn't know what emotion I should be feeling, but I was certainly confused.

"Riley, you don't have to go through things alone. I've always felt safe with you, too. I have never admired anyone the way I admire you and we are going to get through this. Even if…I end up going to jail for murder, I will never forget these last few days."

Riley turned her head and wiped a tear from her eye. "All right, enough with the drama.

Let's go find out about this book."

She was clearly still upset, but I felt it best to leave it be. "You're right," I said. "Sophie? Rev it up!" From somewhere in the backseat, Sophie stuck her hands into the car, and the car engine turned on, roaring loudly. I shifted the car into drive just as Riley leaned over and kissed my cheek quickly. I nearly jerked the wheel right then. I turned and looked at her and I saw her looking out the window, her cheeks clearly flustered. I played it cool and revved the engine a few times. "Hang on, gang."

"Whoo Hoo!" Sophie screamed from the back seat. We tore off into the street. Suddenly, the car started to levitate off the ground. Higher and higher as we cleared the buildings. The wheels were spinning with no traction and a cloud of mist had encompassed the whole vehicle. As the mist cleared below the window I could tell we were soaring over the town.

"Sophie? What are you doing?" I shouted, nervously.

"Ghost things," she said happily.

I looked over at Riley whose face was lit up with glee and admiration. Sophie was getting stronger, and I think she knew it.

"Ghost things," I repeated. "Right, okay then. Let's see what this car can really do!"

I floored it, but Sophie had full control. Her happy cheering rang through our ears as she made the car soar like an eagle through the morning sky.

CHAPTER

THIRTEEN

"GENTLY, gently!" I shouted as the car swept a tree and hovered in front of The Open Page bar. Sophie laughed and the car fell about two feet landing with a snap as the axle to the car broke when we hit the road. "Okay, we will work on your landing."

Sophie laughed and vanished into the backseat. Riley rubbed the back of her head, as she sat up. "Are all ghosts this unpredictable?"

I opened the door and crawled out of the car. "Only the ones that seem to be connected to me." I kicked the hood and the car lurched and suddenly started to smoke. "Do ghosts have insurance?" Riley asked, jokingly.

I turned around trying to spot the little girl. "Let's not forget that we just let an underage drive the car," I remarked. "Come on, let's get inside before we draw even more attention to ourselves." I shoved the leather book under my arm and grabbed Riley by the hand.

Riley and I ran inside the bookstore. Mr. Hunter was staring out the window looking at the smoking car in front of his building. "Mr. Crane? What the hell is going on out there?"

"Oh you know, those crazy Indiana Drivers. Hey, can we ask you a question?"

Mr. Hunter picked up a phone and started dialing 911. Before he could hit the call button, I slammed the book down on the counter as loudly as I could. "It's kinda important, sir."

Mr. Hunter slowly lowered the phone as his gaze went to us, and then back to the book. "What's this all about?"

I stared at him hard and opened the book up to the cover. "This book, Passed Relations, it is one of yours, and I need to know everything you know about this book."

Mr. Hunter's eyes narrowed and he leaned forward on the counter. "I don't know where you found that infernal book, but I will not have it in my bar. Leave."

"Why?" Riley asked urgently. "What's so special about it?"

"Why the hell is it so special to you?" Mr. Hunter was already going to the door, opening it, beckoning us to leave.

"Because someone very special is in need of it and I think it will help them," I said, on the verge of begging.

"What monster could possibly need that book?"

"A…ghost I met."

He let go of the door, and it swung shut with a heavy pound.

"Thomas…you are not bringing this back into my store again, are you? There is no such thing as ghosts."

"Yes there is." Riley stood beside me. "I've seen them. Myself."

Mr. Hunter began to laugh. "Don't tell me he has convinced you of this nonsense. Thomas? You really dragged this sweet girl into this?"

"I volunteered," she said with a sneer.

Mr. Hunter stood there in a stunned silence glancing at her and then back at me. "That book is nothing but trouble, and I want it far away from here."

I stepped forward. "Why? What's wrong with it? It's just a book."

"A book of lies!" He raised his voice, causing me to stop in my tracks. "That book is full of hate and won't bring you anything but trouble."

"But why?" I asked again.

"BECAUSE IT COULDN'T BRING HER BACK!" he shouted.

Riley and I watched as he leaned against the counter and collapsed to the floor. "It couldn't...I tried, and the book couldn't...it's a lie. All of it."

I looked from the book to the sorrowful, sad eyes of Mr. Hunter. "You tried to resurrect your granddaughter, didn't you?"

He never looked at me. He just sat on the ground and tried to hide his tears. "Ghosts aren't real. If they were, she would be here. She would never...she couldn't leave me." He was choking back sobs.

I looked at Riley. She seemed annoyed by his outburst, and I couldn't really blame her. Up until a day ago she had been just as upset as he was about the possibility of ghosts now being real, and now she was in my corner, unable to defend what can't be seen.

"I want you out of my shop. I want you both out right now, and I don't want to see you back here. I can't keep living in a desperate hope that..."

Suddenly a book fell off a shelf. All three of our heads turned and stared at it. Then another fell. And another. The books began to domino off the shelves in a crazy pattern.

"What the hell is going on?" Mr. Hunter questioned.

I turned and smiled at him. "I hate to tell you this, sir, but I'm afraid your shop is haunted."

Riley clasped her hands together. "Is that…?"

"There's the crazy kid." I snapped my fingers and pointed. Sophie was having the time of her life making a mess of the shop.

"How is this possible?" Mr. Hunter was slowly coming to his feet. "What are you…how are you doing this?"

I turned back and crossed my arms with a wink. "This my friend, is Ectomancy. You know, the ability to talk to ghosts? I feel like I told you this before."

Mr. Hunter's eyes were full of, not fear but…astonishment. He took a few steps forward toward the books and spread his arms. "It's…possible I misjudged you."

"You're damn right you did!" Riley chimed in.

He ran his hand through the air, as if trying to feel a breeze or a cool wind in the air. Sophie gave me a puzzled look, and I nodded to her to assure her it was okay. She reached out to him and I could see her brush her fingertips along his hand. He closed his eyes and I noticed him steady his breathing. "Mary?" he whispered softly.

Sophie looked angry, but I held up my hand to silence her. "No, sir. This is Sophia. She is young and new to the whole, well, being dead thing and I think I can help her, but I am going to need your assistance."

Mr. Hunter waved a tear away as he dropped her arm to his side. "I don't know why my granddaughter wouldn't come back to me. I tried everything. All of these useless books and all this voodoo…why would she not want to tell me she was okay?"

I put my hand on his shoulder. "Maybe she couldn't. It's a very complicated dimension. I have talked to many ghosts who don't understand it either, and that is why they feel trapped. Maybe the fact that your granddaughter didn't try to contact you is because…well, she made it."

He turned his head to look at me, and a smile crossed his face. "You may be full of it sometimes Mr. Crane, but you do have heart. I can't deny you that." He paused before solemnly asking, "Do you have any idea who would want to kill her? And leads? Suspects?"

Looking back into my mind palace, which was a series of disorganized filing cabinets with mental food stains, I narrowed it down. "Well, there is my old boss Franklin at the Pretzel shop."

Mr. Hunter lightened up. "Oh, the Twisted Snack Shop? I love those."

I glared at him. Riley raised her hand. "You really think your boss could do something like that?"

I bit my lip. I thought of Simon and how my boss's actions had drawn him to extreme measures. Was he capable of murder? "I don't know, but I sure as hell hate his face."

Mr. Hunter smiled. "Anyone else?"

"Well, there was a screaming entity at her apartment. A shrill female voice that pierced through the air and threw glass at our faces."

Mr. Hunter started taking down notes. "Okay, so we got an entity that only you can see, and a guy that you hate that isn't capable of murder."

"There's you," Riley chimed in.

My eyes glazed over as I snapped my head in her direction.

She shrugged and shook her head. "Well, I mean I know you didn't do it, but let's face it, the clues are kinda all over your face."

"Thank you, Riley…you're very helpful," I said sarcastically.

I thought back to the room with the single light. I thought about the liquor littered floor and the glass strewn about the floor. I thought about the graveyard in the distance. I thought about Sophie.

No…Sophie's father? Would anybody be so cruel as to murder their own daughter? "Sophie? Were you close to your father?" I asked, timidly.

"Father is always angry. Father doesn't seem to like mommy or I. He almost seemed like he wasn't daddy." I didn't think he was the same guy from the fishing trip.

Riley stepped forward from somewhere behind the bar shoving an ale somewhere in her outfit. I dare not ask where. Mr. Hunter did not seem to mind either. "So you'll translate the book?" she asked Hunter.

He flipped through a few pages while Sofia hung over his shoulder. "I'll try. My knowledge of this is probably even weaker than yours to be honest. I think I can grasp the concept of what is good and what is bad in any case."

The sound of tires screeched outside. The clicking of doors sounded from nearby. The voice of a familiar prick echoed through my skull.

"MR CRANE, COME OUT OF THE BOOK STORE WITH YOUR HANDS UP."

The voice came booming from the street. I looked out the window and saw the newly familiar image of red and blue lights outside. Detective Conner was outside with a megaphone in one hand, the other resting on his gunbelt.

"Good," I said to Mr. Hunter. "Because bad seems to be following us around a lot lately."

"COME OUT WITH YOUR HANDS UP! THIS IS YOUR FINAL WARNING."

I looked at Riley who was already hiding behind a bookshelf drinking her ale quickly. I gave her an exasperated look. "What? They don't serve you alcohol in jail, Thomas. I'm not going in sober."

I shook my head. "Come on, Riley. You're good at this, remember? What do we do?"

Riley looked around the shop at the messy displays and fallen books and shrugged. "I don't know this time."

Mr. Hunter raised his hands and approached the door. "Let me talk to him and see what I can do."

I grabbed his shoulder. "Wait. This is my battle, and I am done putting others in harm's way." I looked at Riley. "If I don't come back inside, find a way to help her."

"I can't talk to her the way you can, Thomas. I wouldn't know what to do," she protested.

Riley walked forward and I held my hand up.

"Find a way. I promised her Riley. Please."

I grabbed the handle of the door and opened it slowly, being blinded by the flashlight of Detective Conner. I held my hand up and did what I do best…Let my mouth get me in trouble.

"Is that necessary, sir? It's like five in the afternoon."

"Get on the Ground, now Crane. I'm taking you in."

I raised my hands above my head, but I didn't budge. "I didn't do it, Detective. I have committed no crime."

"You escaped from custody in the back of my squad car," he snapped.

I opened my mouth and quickly closed it. Damn it. "Okay, yeah, but only because you arrested an innocent man."

"You mean the man I found at the crime scene over the body of a deceased girl and who ran away from law enforcement? That innocent man?"

"…Yeah?" Damn it…he was good.

Detective Conner came up to me and removed his handcuffs from his belt before turning me around and snapping them on my wrist. The cold steel felt uncomfortably familiar. I shouldn't have been surprised when he made them extra tight.

"You have the right to remain silent, anything you do or say will be subject to…"

"Yeah yeah yeah, I know the drill," I interrupted. "Get ready to have a documentary of details that no one wants to hear or listen to because of the freak who speaks to ghosts now being captive. Congrats, Detective."

I think he took my sarcastic remarks as actual praise because he seemed to be incredibly happy as I narrated his success. I got placed into the backseat of the car aggressively, while the door seemed to slam behind me instantaneously. I looked out the window and saw Mr. Hunter, Sofia, and Riley staring at me from the door. Mr. Hunter held the book tightly and turned around back toward the bar. I saw Sophia look down at the ground as she faded away in the light. And Riley…she took one step outside just as the car began to drive away, allowing her to fade farther and farther away into the distance. She never stopped looking at the car.

I sat in silence contemplating the last few days. I'd failed the little girl, but that didn't mean the case was over. Riley was smart and she would figure something out. And she had Mr. Hunter. He was very new to this as well but he had the intellect and the know-how on the references. I at least assume he watched a movie or two about ghosts. They were going to be fine. Right? Oh fuck, I gotta get out of here and help them.

"You're a real nutcase aren't you Crane?" Conner finally spoke through the grated screen in the car.

"That's what they tell me," I said, staring out the window.

"So, intrigue me, Casper. That's what they call you, right?"

"Sometimes."

"Right. The ghost whisperer. So answer me this. If you didn't kill that Sophia Brownstone, who did?"

I laid my head against the glass. "I wish I knew."

I could see Conner's devilish smile through the rearview mirror. It killed me inside that his sarcastic grin was better than mine. "Surely you can see why all signs point to you?" I actually nodded. I couldn't think of a valid argument. Not this time.

Conner continued. "We are going to get you back to the station and release Gary Brownstone. I think he has been interrogated enough. I knew he had nothing to do with it."

I raised my head. "You have her father?"

"For now," he continued. "Got a few more questions for him before we book you for murder."

I frowned. "What did he say exactly?"

There was that smirk again. "I don't have to tell you anything about the case, but seeing as how you're already captured I don't see why not. We called him after we found the body. Poor thing. He rushed over and you should have seen his face."

I could feel my head start to throb. "What idiot leaves a girl that young all alone in an apartment while you're away?"

Conner laughed. "That shows how much you know, Crane. She wasn't alone. She had a babysitter watching her."

My eyes started to hurt. "He is lying. There was no one else there when she died."

Conner scoffed. "You would know, wouldn't you, Mister Home Intruder. I agree he doesn't seem to be all there, most of this town's drunks aren't. The guy nearly drank himself into a coma one time. Man kept babbling about a shadow person in his house. It sounded crazy to me but he passed the lie detector test."

I felt sick. "But that's impossible."

"No, that's science. What's impossible is you being able to speak to ghosts."

I fidgeted in the car. This was crazy. Who the hell was watching the little girl then?

Conner got on his car radio and began to recite a phrase I'm sure he spent the last few days rehearsing in his mirror. "I have Thomas Crane. I will be bringing him to lock up in about…"

It was replaced by horrible feedback and the static hurt my ears. "Stupid thing. This is Detective Conner, do you copy? Over."

All the lights in the front of the car went out before flicking back on in rapid succession.

"What the hell?" Conner clicked his radio a few times and got no response. "Stupid system. They just updated this and it's already on the fritz? Repeat, this is Detective Conner, I am bringing in murder suspect…"

The steering wheel lurched from his hands and the car spun to the left hard, smacking my head against the door. It jumped the curb and ran along the street flipping over a garbage can. The car lurched back onto the road and turned around one hundred and eighty degrees before flooring it in reverse.

"WHAT THE FUCK IS GOING ON?" Conner screamed.

He couldn't hear it, but the sound of a little girl was laughing joyfully from somewhere in the console. Now it was my turn to have the annoying smirk. "What's wrong, Detective? Forget to renew your driver's license?"

The car began to wail its sirens on again and off again. Conner forced the wheel and regained control, slamming on the break. The car came to a screeching halt. He checked his dash cam, but it had died with the blackout. He tried to turn around but the car jumped into the air about ten feet and started to slowly spin.

"PUT ME DOWN!" he shouted, gripping the steering wheel tightly. "PUT THIS CAR DOWN THIS INSTANCE!"

I really wish my hands weren't tied behind my back. "You had to say instance, didn't you?"

The car dropped hard and fast as it smashed into the ground, hood up. The airbags deployed in the front of the cab as the car sat for a split second before tumbling onto its roof. The sound of the sirens beeped into a toneless squeal as the car came to a stop.

"Detective?" I managed to say through broken glass and twisted metal. "I would like to reopen my case."

Conners groaned and I could see his arm flex behind the dented steel grate. I can't be for certain, but I am pretty sure he was giving me the finger. The sound of Sophie's voice was the most beautiful sound I'd heard all day.

CHAPTER
FOURTEEN

STUMBLING out of the car I checked my body for scratches or broken bones, or as best I could with my hands still behind my back. Two days in a row I'd been in a car accident. I don't think a man my age should be in three this early in life. Either someone out there is looking out for me, or someone is really bad at trying to kill me.

"I saved you, Thomas!" Sophia shouted from behind me.

"Yes you did, girl. Again. I thought I was the one who was supposed to be the hero." Sophia put her hands behind her back and started swaying from side to side. "Come on, we should probably get out of here before…"

I was interrupted as a heatwave crashed over me. I looked toward the police car which was now suddenly engulfed in flames.

"Ow, I can't move. My leg is trapped."

"Detective?" I asked into the growing flame. "Hang on, I'll figure something out." I went to reach for the door, but my hands were tightly bound. I turned around and tried to get closer but the flames were growing fast and getting hotter.

"HELP" I shouted out into the sky.

I looked around and there was no one in sight, not even the evening traffic.

"Really? You had to drop us into the dead part of town?"

Sophia didn't respond. She seemed fixated on the building fire.

"HELP!" Conner shouted. "I can't breathe." He was coughing through the smoke.

"Sophia? Do you think you can?"

Sophia looked up at me with confused eyes. "Help him? But he wanted to put you away."

"Yes, and if we don't help him I may be put away for two murders."

"What if I can't?"

I crouched down beside her. "Please Sophia. What would your mother want you to do?"

I could hear Conner cough again. "Who are you speaking to, Thomas?"

"Your guardian angel. Now hold on."

Sophia had a look of determination and glided over to the police door. She reached her hand out for the handle, her mist skin ignoring the flame. She held her breath and touched the door handle and it passed through.

"Thomas, I don't think I can."

I was beginning to have a hard time breathing as well. "Sofia, please. Do it for us. Do it to save someone's life."

I saw a physical connection as Sophia seemed to grow brighter, her hand reaching around the dented car door, pulling it off the car. And I don't just mean she opened the car door, she threw it down the street like some ravaged beast. She shifted into the car, phasing through the torn machinery and flame and seconds later I saw Conner being pulled from the wreckage. To the naked eye, it would have looked like he was flying on his own. Sophia placed him gently on the ground several feet away from the fiery inferno and gave me a look of contempt.

"Is he going to be alright?"

It was the first time I could remember Sohpia saying something so selfless. She pulled a man who deposed her friends from a flaming vehicle. They really do grow up so fast don't they?

Conner coughed again, his face was dirty and his head was badly scarred. "You mind telling me what happened exactly?"

I felt the click of my handcuffs as they fell to the street. Sophia had nabbed the keys from Conner's pocket. Sophia came around and started spinning the keys around her little finger. To Conner, his ring of keys was hovering over his face, ridiculing him.

"Well Conner, let me tell you a ghost story."

CONNER, Sophia and I went to a nearby coffee house. He ordered a highly caffeinated drink while I ordered a soda. It had been too long since I had something that wasn't jail house food or fear in my throat. Conner began to stir several spoonfuls of sugar into his coffee, his hand shaking violently against the glass. He wrapped his hands around the mug and I could tell he was jittery even before his first sip.

I began to explain to him about my ability, and about Sophia, and about all the events leading up to the latest in car crashes. (Seriously I should not have so many on my list.)

After a long moment he sipped his coffee again, the mug tinkering against his teeth. "So…ghosts are real?"

I sighed. "Really Leroy? Yes! After all that, THAT's what you take away from this?"

He didn't make eye contact, but he nodded rapidly. "It's kinda a big deal."

I sipped my soda. I guess that was a fair point. They can't all have the steel cajones that Riley had had. Detective Conner lived in the real world. The supernatural was merely a fairy tale. And now his eyes were opening that maybe…okay, yeah, I guess it is a lot to take in.

Detective Conner blinked a few times and began looking around the diner. "So are there any ghosts around here?"

I couldn't help but laugh. "Just Sophie." He seemed to jump at that.

"And where exactly is she?" he asked timidly.

"Sitting beside you." His eyes darted to the empty spot next to him.

"And what is she doing?"

I looked at Sophia and winked. "She is doing the whole, I'm not touching you thing next to your face." Conner visibly scooted a bit toward the window seat.

"I didn't like…go through her right?"

"That depends, did you feel cold?" I joked.

"I don't know…maybe? Damn, is she okay? I can move." He jumped to the other side of the bench and stood up so fast his coffee spilled.

"You're fine, Detective, I'm fucking with you. She is a ghost, you can't hurt her I promise."

He seemed disturbed by that. "But she can hurt me?"

I grinned. "Only if you're bad."

He pinched the bridge of his nose and breathed heavily. "Okay, I gotta report this. Hold tight."

I suddenly got paranoid. "Report what, man? I thought you were on my side now?"

"I gotta report the crashed police car and say that…I don't know, I can't say you escaped again."

"You could say I died and really freak everybody out back at the station. Then they believe in ghosts, right?" I was really enjoying getting under his skin. He actually did seem to consider it for a moment, though.

"I'll figure it out later. Right now, we need to get back to the station. I think I got some further questions to ask Sophia's father."

Sophia looked nervous. "Thomas, you don't really think my daddy would kill me do you?"

I couldn't look at her. "I can't be for certain. He seems really unstable."

Conner looked at me confused. "Oh, you're talking to the ghost, huh? Oh, this is gonna take some getting used to."

"Welcome to the club, Ace." I reached out my hand. He clasped it, but he pulled me close.

"You're not off the hook yet. Just because you proved you're not a fraud, I still haven't completely ruled you out."

I grimaced as his hand tightened. I can't win.

Out the window, I saw Riley and Mr. Hunter wandering the streets looking around frantically. Mr. Hunter's grip was fastened to the book. They seemed distressed and uneasy. I was about to go out to the street to wave her down when Conner grabbed my arm pulling me back into the diner.

"You know that girl?"

I stopped and turned. "You mean the girl who looks like a Victorian modern day electric goth model who fell from heaven and has graced us with her alternative dark ways?"

Conner looked at me, blinking unevenly.

"Nope," I said. "Never seen her before."

His face fell. "She spraypainted my face and broke you out of my car."

I pulled away from him. "Yeah, well you deserved it. Now come on. She may have news about the book."

"Ah yes, the book of divine evil wizardry," he grumbled.

"Look, you accept ghosts, but not magic? Priorities man."

I walked out into the street and waved at Riley and Mr. Hunter. They saw us and sprinted over, slowing down as she recognized Conner. "What the actual fuck is he doing here? And why are you not in handcuffs? And why are you all scratched up? And why…?"

"You can ask Sophie later, Riley. It's good to see you, too."

She stared at Conner suspiciously. "And what's to stop him from just arresting us again when we do something he doesn't like?"

"And what are you going to be doing that I don't like?" he retorted.

"Oh I got a backpack full of spray paint that I would be more than happy to…"

"Okay," I interrupted. "Enough playtime you guys. Time for crime solving. Mr. Hunter, have you learned anything new from between those pages?"

Mr. Hunter scrolled through some pages that he had already bookmarked. "I actually learned quite a bit. Like did you know that ghosts have a severe hatred of salt due to its purity and on this level of…"

"Okay, that's great. Does it say anything about how to find the source of one's death?" Riley interrupted.

Mr. Hunter glared but he flipped through a few more pages. "It says that any ghost who is trapped and does not know why or how she died is because she lacks the knowledge of the source."

"English Professor," Conner said, pinching his nose.

"She doesn't believe she was murdered because she was never educated on what death truly is."

I turned to Sophie who was sitting on the curb trying to pick up a rock, to no avail.

"Sophie, how did you say your mother died?"

Sophie stopped moving, almost as if someone had hit a pause button on her. She spoke slowly and with hope. "My mommy didn't die. She got sick. She got really sick. And daddy said that she needed sleep. One day while I was out playing, daddy said she got taken away, to be in a better place. I thought that…I always thought that…"

Riley touched my arm as she saw tears begin to swell in my eyes. I looked around and everyone was looking at me with curiosity plastered all over their faces. Sophie looked up at me with a look, but it was a haunting look. One that no longer had innocence, or childlike wonder. She looked like she was opening her eyes for the very first time.

"My mommy is gone, isn't she?"

I couldn't help it. I dropped to my knees and tried desperately to give her a hug. "Yes, Sophie. But you can see her again. I mean, you should both be…you should be able to…"

Damn it, who was I kidding? Over twenty years I've had this ability and I still didn't know what the fuck I was talking about or what could or couldn't happen. I was as clueless as the ghost before me.

"Mr. Hunter," I said, wiping my eyes. "Is there any way that we can find her mother? Is there a way for us to get Sophie to see her mother?"

Mr Hunter flipped more pages. "It says that the best way is to have the two together. Sophie must be near her mother to make contact with her, even on the spiritual plane. Do we know where her mother is?"

I exchanged glances with Riley. "You think that was the phenomenon we had when we were wandering around Sophie's apartment? That ghostly wail and the glass that tried to staple us to the wall?"

I could tell Conner was trembling with either rage or embarrassment. Or both. That had not been his brightest day.

"It would make sense," Riley said. "Didn't you say whatever made that sound disappeared from the window?"

I nodded. It had been a very disturbing experience to say the least. I could still feel the cold air on my skin.

Mr. Hunter flipped more pages, pushing his glasses up to his eyes. "How do we find a ghost that doesn't want to be found?"

Conner closed his eyes and I could tell he was debating on telling us something. He ran his fingers through his hair and pinched his nose again. Clearly this was becoming a coping mechanism. "I think I know who you can talk to. The…little girl's…father is still in interrogation. I think I maybe…maybe…can get you clearance to talk to him."

"See Detective? You can be one of the good guys, too!" I said, cheekily.

He furrowed his brow. "I'm a cop, Casper. I'm meant to be the good guy. It's people like you who are twisting us into whatever this gang of misfits is."

Riley laughed. "Fine, you can be the rebel. Never thought I'd be on this side of the law."

Conner frowned. "Let's get something straight right now, you're not cops. This is a tricky situation and I am bringing you in as a guest to help with the investigation. Don't go getting carried away. I could lose my license if I start falling into the game of 'ghosts are real.'"

"Not fun being the nutcase who speaks to ghosts is it, Leroy?" I wanted my words to hit home, and to my own credit they did. I took his long drawn out silence as an answer.

And what a gang of misfits it was. A cop, a book keeper, a goth girl, a ghost, and me...the freak translator. Oh the police force is in for one crazy night.

My mind was filled with so many emotions. I wanted so badly to help Sophie. Her kindness and uncertainty of the world was heartbreaking. Not only was she uncertain of the real world but her own as well. I tried to put myself into the mind of her father. If he was the killer, why would he harm his own daughter? Was the mom truly sick, or was that another murder under her old man's belt? He had to have killed her, right? My anger toward this man grew and grew with each step toward the station.

Our ragtag group entered through the heavy doors and into the lobby. It was surprisingly dark and not very inviting. When I had been brought in before under suspicion of murder, it had all been a blur. I didn't even remember the decaying flower on the secretary's desk, the dark encompassing walls where the shadows danced mindlessly to no rhythm, the gently shimmering lights overhead slowly going in and out…wait a minute.

I leaned over to Riley and whispered gently. "I don't think we are alone here."

Riley nodded. "Good. You see it too. I was beginning to think I'd had my own near death experience and was going crazy."

"Yeah, well if you do, tell me. I am pretty sure you would be better at this than I am."

Riley nudged me. "You think it's the same ghost from the apartment?"

"Could be," I agreed. "And if it's who I think it is, she will not be happy that we are here." I glanced at Sophie who kept looking around. It was almost like she felt a familiar presence in the air. She seemed scared.

Conner led us into a dark hallway opposite the station. We passed by the interrogation booth and inside we could see an old man, ratted and dirty, sitting opposite an empty chair. His face was down on his arms on the table, but I knew this was our man.

"Wait here," Conner demanded. "You will be able to see and hear everything, but it's soundproof from this side. Don't even think of interfering with this interrogation. Understand?"

We all nodded. Conner looked around at the ground pretty aimlessly. "And don't let…that…anywhere near her father. We don't need spooks on top of creeps." Sophie stuck her tongue out at him, but she remained planted in place. "The station will be on a tight lock down while you are here, in case you try anything funny." Conner eyed the group suspiciously.

"Go do your job, Detective. You know best, right?" I said, smartly.

He nodded and rounded the corner of the hall. Pretty sure he didn't realize I was being sarcastic.

CHAPTER
SIXTEEN

I stood in the musky hallway with Riley and Sophie watching Mr. Brownstone. Detective Conner entered the room, a clipboard under his arm and a look of professionalism drowning over him. Gary looked up and eyed the Detective coldly. He clearly had been through this routine a few times.

Detective Conner straightened his outfit. He had apparently gone to a sink and washed his face because the scratch on his head was merely a mark now. His hair was combed back and he was wearing some new crisp clothes. He looked good. I felt Riley tense up as she watched him walk toward the empty chair sitting down heavily. I swear I heard her sigh slightly.

Cops, am I right?

"Your name is Gary Brownstone, am I right?" Conner surveyed his notes, already knowing the answer. Gary's eyes were sunken in and he looked like he hadn't eaten or drank anything in days. Perhaps he hadn't. Gary was staring at the cold steel table, expressionless as Conner sat in the chair across from him, his own steely gaze unblinking as he tried to get inside the mind of this possible killer.

"So you are acutely aware that you are the number one suspect of the death of a Sophie Brownstone. Anything you would like to say to that?"

Gary tapped his foot aggressively. His eyes were closed and I got the sinking suspicion he wanted to be anywhere other than here.

"Sophie is your daughter then, yeah?" Conner broke the silence, intertwining his fingers and laying them on the table.

Gary Brownstone said nothing.

"You of course have the right to remain silent, but if I were you I'd start talking. There have been many murders in the area lately, and I'd hate to have to pin them all on one person. Don't you think it would be smart to defend yourself?"

Silence.

"So why did you kill her?" he asked.

Silence again.

"You're really not gonna talk to me are you?"

Gary looked up. "There is nothing to say. You have made your choice."

Conner nodded. "Perhaps. Or perhaps my eyes have opened up to other possibilities in the world." He glanced over at the two-way mirror at me. "We can't know everything, can we Mr. Brownstone?"

He looked up at Conner, his stare waning.

"Let's change the subject, then," Conner said, crossing his legs. "You left your daughter alone the night she died?"

He looked toward the wall at the two-way mirror where we sat watching. He seemed to look right through the glass. "I would never leave her alone without supervision."

Conner made a note. "We checked the house, Mr Brownstone. There was nobody there."

"I assure you there was."

"All right then, Gary. Can I call you Gary? Who was the babysitter on that fateful night?" Gary looked back at Conner as if he wanted to leap across the table.

"No. You don't get to bring her into this."

Conner leaned forward. "Who?"

"My wife, you blue collared bastard."

Conner's eyes narrowed and he looked back at his notes. "It says here that your wife is dead, Mr Brownstone. Care to elaborate?"

His stare never moved, but his lips pursed with a vengeful snarl. "I did not murder my daughter, Detective."

"Well, be that as it may, you certainly left her alone and for that we can charge you with child neglect. Would you like that Gary? To know you left her all alone to die?" Gary gently struggled in his seat, clearly uncomfortable.

Conner stood up, putting the clipboard under his arm as he walked toward the door. "Clearly you have made your case clear. Wait here till I get back."

Conner came and joined us in the hallway, a look of certainty across his face. "I don't know how he managed to dodge the lie detector test before. I am pretty sure he at least believes he didn't do it."

I stared at Gary. He was a very sad man. For such a large human he looked so small. He had lost his wife and daughter, and had clearly lost himself to drink. So why did I still not believe he killed her? Why did I believe in his innocence?

"I don't like it, Conner. Something still seems off."

Conner shrugged. "I don't really like it either, but clues are clues and this appears to be a guilty man. The man is a drunk and a bad father."

I glared at him. "Just like how I was guilty till proven innocent?"

Conner glared back but he didn't respond. He walked past me and into a nearby office, with Gary's folder tucked under his arm.

I turned to look at Sophia. Tears were swelling in her eyes as she stared at her father behind the glass. Gary sat motionless, and then, he started to sob. He folded in on himself on the steel table and began crying hysterically.

"Oh Sophia, I am so sorry. I am sorry I wasn't strong enough. I am sorry that you fell!" He buried his face into his arms and wept openly and loudly. I looked at Riley who had a look of heartbreak, a single tear escaping her heavily mascara eyes. I turned to look at Sophie, who had put her ghostly hand against the glass, resistance falling upon her hand as her fingers curled against the panel. A physical force. A link.

"Detective…I don't think he did it," I managed to whisper.

"What are you talking about?" Conner groaned.

Sophie phased through the glass and glided delicately over to her father. She hovered for a minute before leaning forward and hugging him tightly, and to my surprise, Gary seemed to feel it. He stopped crying just long enough as Sophia whispered in his ear, "I love you Daddy. I forgive you."

Gary sat up, and looked around. He started rapidly drying his eyes as Sophia disappeared again in a cloud of mist behind him.

"Sophia?" he gasped aloud as her figure turned to mist before his eyes. Had Gary heard her? Was there a connection so strong that Sophia had broken the ghost dimension?

Sophia appeared beside Riley and I shortly after. We looked at Gary one last time who seemed to be composing himself. That's the power of love, man. Even death can't stand between it.

Mr. Hunter, Riley, Sophia, and I started heading back to the police station lobby.

"So what now?" Mr. Hunter asked.

I kept walking with my head hung low. "I don't know. I figured once we got this far we would have more answers, but I feel like we are stuck with even more questions."

"Thomas, I don't think my daddy did it. I don't think he would ever really hurt me."

I reached for Sophia's hand but she either was too distraught or wasn't focusing. "Sophia, your dad drinks a lot and that doesn't make his brain work too good. He may have made a mistake but he still is responsible somehow. Right, Riley?"

Riley didn't answer. I don't think she knew what to say.

"Well, I don't think he did it," Sophia declared.

I looked to the floor. "You know, Sophia, I am starting to believe you."

"Thomas, you can't be serious. Conner is right, all signs point to…who the hell is that?"

Sophie stopped in her tracks. Riley and Mr. Hunter looked up, speaking almost simultaneously "Who?"

I looked at my friends in surprise. What did they mean they couldn't see it? There in the center of the police station lobby stood a very tall and old man. He had a long white beard, and was wearing a long black cloak. His eyes were featureless, but I think the thing that made him stand out the most was a long iron sword he had equipped to his hip.

I blinked. "You don't see the guy that looks like he stepped out of a Wizard movie?"

Sophia hid behind me. "He is scary."

Riley and Mr. Hunter looked around, clearly not seeing what we saw.

I eyed Riley skeptically. The figure caught me off guard. Not only could Riley not see him, I couldn't see through him. Everything that this ability had taught me was that I had the ability to see through the spectral form of a spirit. Never once had I met a spirit that had appeared…solid.

What was this guy?

The cloaked figure walked toward us, towering over with his exceptional height. "It is time," he said with an elderly voice that was equally terrifying.

"It's time for what?" I asked, trying not to show my trembling fear.

"The journey is over for the lost soul, and I have come to collect," the cloak said. It was gentle but something about this fellow told me he could kick my ass. For once, I thought it suitable to keep my big sarcastic mouth shut.

"Who are you?" I asked, looking him up and down, his features almost appeared skeletal as he lifted his hand to the hilt of his sword.

"I have no name, for I am a Warden of Death, and time is up."

My blood ran cold. The Warden of Death had been in the books I'd read. Death comes for us all and it's not all heavenly hands and clouds. Death comes to us as a being, and this was one of many.

I was standing face to face with a Reaper.

I put my arm up to shield my friends. Riley started hugging herself. She acted cold. "Thomas? What is happening?"

I raised my hand toward the Reaper. "I don't know who sent you, but I am not ready to go yet and neither are my friends. Please go away."

The reaper leaned forward, his skeletal features appeared more shadowed. "You do not wish to mess with the balance of things more than you already have. I could tell you and your friend there right now when you will die and how, but that is not my mission."

I scoffed. "So what? You are the bender of free will? I like to think I make my own choices…sir."

Riley took a few steps backwards. "Thomas, what the hell is going on?"

I put up my hand to calm her. "We don't want what you're selling, Bonehead."

The reaper reached out his hand and a gust of strong cold wind flew through me. I looked back and Riley appeared to be experiencing it also. I looked at Sophie, but she was being dragged toward the Reaper. Some unseen force had her in his grip.

"Sophie! Let her GO!"

"I have come to collect. All that can be done has been done." The Reaper's cloak then opened up and I could hear screaming. Like the gates of hell had opened up and within his cloak were thousands of souls captured in his cloth. Sophia reached out a hand. She was screaming for me but I couldn't hear her, the freezing mist was too strong.

"Please, you can't do this. You can't."

The Reaper held Sophia in one hand. He appeared to have grown two sizes. "And why shouldn't I? Her path is closed."

"Because LOOK AT HER!" I screamed. "She is just a child! Her life has barely begun and you're taking her away!"

The Reaper didn't move. "And so is life. It comes, and goes, and we must make the collection. Why is she any different?"

"Because I promised her!" I said, bowing my head.

The Reaper stared at me for a long while. "You are Thomas Crane. One of many to escape my hand. Had it not been for divine intervention, you would be within my grasp at not much older than this young girl. What makes you fit to make promises to the deceased?"

I looked up. "I don't know. I feel like I owe her, do I not? Just because she is dead doesn't mean she doesn't need guidance."

The Reaper studied the girl and closed his cloak but he held her tightly above the ground. "I ask you again. Why? Why does this concern you?"

I crouched below the mighty being. "Because I promised her I'd get her answers. Please. You must spare her."

The Reaper put the girl back on the ground but wrapped his long bony fingers around her shoulders. "This girl is dead. There is nothing more you can do to bring her back. Her body is all but destroyed and you cannot change that. As is death. I ask you one last time. WHY?"

His voice boomed through the hallway to the point where I think even Riley and Mr. Hunter heard him. They were huddled close, staring at me with terror.

I found myself fighting tears. I had to say something. "Because…I know what it's like to die and come back alone and scared."

The Reaper turned away from me. "A noble sacrifice. One who has fought death and won, fighting to help one who fought death and lost. I see your value, however this changes nothing. She has her answers, therefore her mission is complete. We must…"

"Give me twenty four hours," I said quickly.

The Reaper looked thoughtful. "But she has already found…"

"To say good-bye," I blurted out.

The Reaper released Sophia who stood there in a paralyzed state. The Reaper's voice boomed as he turned to a shadowy green mist. "Death has a strict curfew, Crane. She has already been exposed for too long."

Sophie spoke up, timid and frightened. "Please Sir. They are my friends."

The Reaper looked down at her and smiled a boney toothy grin. "And you will fight another day to be with them?" he asked her, as a grandfather would a granddaughter.

Sophie nodded. "I love him. I love them all."

The Reaper stood, a dark cloudy mist covering him from the waist down. "You have twenty four hours, Thomas. Do not waste this time. Sophie, I'll be seeing you soon."

I stood up and wiped my eyes as Sophie ran and gave me a hug. A genuine hug. It felt so warm despite her cold exterior. Sophie was becoming stronger, and we had just talked our way into another day. The Reaper had sparred us.

The cold had left icicles upon my eyelashes. I looked at Riley who stood confused, cold, and irritated. "You gonna tell me what I missed?"

"Well, Death itself is watching us, and he has given us a time limit," I said, shaking.

"Death? As in like the Grim Reaper?" Mr. Hunter clung to his book.

"Oh great. And here I thought it was going to be something bad." Riley closed her eyes, annoyed. "What do you mean Death is watching us?"

I looked at Sophia, her eyes still large with fear. "I don't have time to explain. Not right now. Can you get us a car, Riley?"

Riley perked up. "A police station on lockdown with a garage full of abandoned vehicles? I'll think of something."

"No." Conner came around the corner escorting Gary, his hands behind his back. Gary's head was hung low and his eyes were shut. He had been through so much the last few days.

"You are not taking another vehicle, Miss Blake. Have I made myself clear?"

Riley didn't answer, nor did she look deterred. She looked fixated, watching Conner as he got closer to us. I gave Riley a suspicious glance and turned away. The last thing I needed to start getting was jealous. Damn hormones.

Mr. Hunter approached Conner first. "We won't go out of our way to break the law, Detective, but you have to admit this all seems strange. I mean we are trying to help this little girl and just because you and I can't see…"

"Sophie?" a raspy voice said from behind Conner. Gary's eyes had gotten huge and he was staring at Sophie. No, DIRECTLY at Sophie. He struggled in his cuffs and broke free of Conner's grasp. He staggered over to Sophie and dropped to his knees. He saw her. He truly saw her. "Oh Sophie, my baby girl. I am so sorry. I wondered if I would be able to see you the way I did your mother but I never knew. I'm so sorry."

Conner, Riley, and Mr. Hunter all looked at him talking to complete air exchanging glances, all of them stood with their jaws open or biting their lip. I however saw the awkward embrace of a father who lost his daughter, who was framed for her murder, seeing his daughter as a ghost and being weak at the sight of his once-deceased child. It was the most beautiful, yet morbid thing I had ever witnessed.

I had no choice but to step forward. "Mr. Brownstone. I must speak to you."

Gary didn't look at me. He could not take his gaze off his daughter, I presume for fear of losing her again. "Why? So you can call me crazy too? My daughter is here and I must see her before she is gone forever, just like her mother was."

I kneeled down beside him. "I know, Mr. Brownstone. You have a very beautiful daughter."

"Don't patronize me, just let me have this moment with her before it's gone again."

"I'm not patronizing you, sir. I know your daughter has beautiful blonde hair, and a smile that can light a room. She is kind, and selfless, and...a good friend."

Sophie gave me a look, her eyes began to swell, her smile never fading.

"You don't know anything. You could have seen that in the case files. Now stop pestering me and go…"

"His name is Thomas, daddy. And he is just like you," she said,

Gary gasped and looked at me. "So how…you can see…?"

"I also know that her mother made her that pretty blue dress. It is her favorite color after all."

Gary stood up. He eyed me for a long moment before he leaned forward, resting his head on my shoulder. "Thank you. Thank you so much for letting me see her again." I patted his back, unsure of exactly what was going on.

"Hang on a second, Gary," Conner said. "This doesn't explain anything. What do you mean you can see her? Thomas?"

I backed away from Gary, and let him go back to seeing his daughter. "He has the same ability as I do, Detective. That means…Gary, you had a near death experience didn't you?

Gary bent and kissed the top of Sophie's head, which I am sure looked awkward to everyone else. "You could say that."

I smiled. "Detective Conner, I'd like an opportunity to interrogate the suspect, please." This time Conner shook things up. Instead of pinching the bridge of his nose, he just put his whole face in his hands. "Just do what you gotta do."

"What did you do Gary? You have to tell me everything." Gary hesitated, and then bowed his head again in shame. "There is no one here that is going to judge you, man. I have been where you are. If you are going to talk to anybody, it should be me."

Gary spoke up. "You've been where I am, have you? You lost your wife? Your daughter? You have been driven to the point of no return where all you want to do is drink and drink in hopes of forgetting them but you can't?"

I put my hand on his shoulder. "Well, I never had a wife or daughter. I did however lose my father and my mother in a car accident many years ago."

He looked at me with the most human eyes I'd seen on him. "I…I'm sorry."

"What happened, Gary?" I tried to sound as gentle as I could.

He stared at his daughter who had sat next to us on a nearby bench. She was getting better at manipulating objects. Much better. She started playing with her hair as she watched us.

"I love my family," he began. "When my wife got sick, I tried everything to help her get better. I worked extra shifts, I never slept, I even prayed. When she died, I drank. I know it wasn't the right thing to do but I drank and I drank a lot to the point where I blacked out."

"You drank yourself to death?"

I shifted in my seat. My father had also been a fan of the drink but he never got that bad. I suddenly had images of him, memories that I had had as a child where he would smile at me and we would go for walks outside and play catch. I thought of Simon. The ghost that had committed suicide in order to no longer feel the pain of losing his wife to my disgusting boss. I thought of right, and I thought of wrong, and I thought about all the things in between that many would never experience. That solid line between life and death. And my ability, just like

Gary's, was punishment. It was then that I wondered…what did I do in a past life to deserve such a curse. "So what happened next?"

"What happened was Sophie saved my life. She called the cops, just like we taught you, right Sophie?" Sophie smiled and patted her dad's lap.

"Of course! Dial 911 till the illness is done!"

Gary laughed. "That's right. When the cops got there, it was too late, in a matter of speaking. I was in a deep coma, and not breathing. They took me away and got me fixed up. I took meetings, went through child protective services until I was able to come home again and be with my daughter. And that's when…she appeared."

I finally understood. "Your wife?"

"Mm hm," he said. "She was very angry with me but she forgave me. She told me she loved me and that she would always be watching over us. She made me promise not to tell Sophie that a ghost was watching over her. I thought it silly at the time, but I guess she wouldn't have understood."

I nodded. "It can be a lot to take in, a girl that young being told her mother was taking care of her from the afterlife." I looked at Sophie. She, too, was hearing this story for the first time and she looked rather upset.

"But, you told me mommy was sleeping. By the field with the stones!"

Gary looked at her solemnly. "She is, Sweetheart. Your mother is sleeping soundly."

"You said she was trying to get better!"

Gary swallowed. I did, but…"

"YOU SAID I WOULD SEE HER AGAIN!"

"I tried!" Gary pleaded. "I got my hands on this book that was supposed to help resurrect your mother. I wanted us to be a family again."

Suddenly all the lights went out as the bulbs overhead burst. Glass rained down on myself and my friends. They ducked for cover as Conner led everyone up against the wall. I looked at Sophie who was floating above her father, and she was glowing a toxic blue color I had only seen one other time...the cold chill from the apartment bedroom.

"Sophie..." I said calmly.

I looked at Mr. Hunter who was scrolling through the book. "Hey, Thomas...I think we have a problem here."

"HOW DID I DIE, DAD? TELL ME?"

The words struck him hard. It was the first time she had ever referred to him as 'dad' instead of 'daddy.' He looked legitimately hurt.

"HOW DID I DIE?" she repeated, her voice coming across almost like static.

"Your mother and I had a fight, Sophie. Parents do that sometimes. I got mad...and I went out to..."

"To get another drink?" I asked.

He didn't look at me. He couldn't. He was too terrified and captivated by Sophie's new appearance. I gotta admit, I was glad I wasn't on Sophie's bad side. I'd seen her annoyed, even mad, but this? This was a nightmare.

"I'm sorry Sophie," he whispered.

"You just let your daughter stay home alone?" Riley asked, putting the story together.

Gary looked at her innocently. "She wasn't alone. She had...her mother. I told Sophie that if she ever missed her mother, to go to the window and look out at the stones on the hill and there she could talk to her."

Sophie's light grew dimmer but still a static chain erupted from her as she spoke.

"But, my mother didn't hear me…so I leaned closer, and closer until…"

Gary struggled in his cuffs. "Your mother told me she tried to save you but you phased through her hand. You fell Sophie, and…and I wasn't there to save you."

"THOMAS!" Mr. Hunter screamed.

"What, Hunter?" I shouted, exasperated.

"When he tried to resurrect her, all spirits tied to a chain of vengeance of a loved one are incapable of returning to this plane as a physical form of…"

"Oh come on, man! English!" shouted Conner, over the building sounds of wind howling.

Sophie's light grew brighter. That yellow spark turned into a storm as a wild shape of energy came from the top of Sophie's head. The light began to form into the sight of a shapely woman wearing what appeared to be a nightgown as fingers that were long and sickly grasped the neck of Gary and lifted him in the air, his hands cuffed unable to defend himself against the towering spirit.

"He didn't resurrect his wife as a material form, he transformed her into a…"

"YOU LET MY BABY GIRL DIE!" the spirit screamed, the voice a blazing combination of wind, and sound that shoved everything in the hall up against the wall including us.

"HE TURNED HER INTO A BANSHEE!" Mr. Hunter screamed.

Everyone watched as Mr. Brownstone kicked and tried to scream out, but his voice was guttural beneath the strong grasp of his deceased wife's hand. She flung his body down the hall and it skidded to a halt as he smashed against the steel wall.

"Gary!" I cried out. I ran to his side and helped him to his feet. "Conner, get over here and help me with these cuffs!"

Conner dropped and crawled toward me as the lights began shaking and glass from the two way mirror began to crack. Riley ran and jumped over him helping me get Gary to his feet. Mr. Hunter crouched down and went to Conner to help him across, covering his head with the book.

"Is this what you meant by 'death is watching us', Thomas?" Riley asked, shielding her face with her arm.

"No, that was another supernatural force of the unknown," I replied.

Riley smirked. "And they said you were bad at making friends."

The Banshee's scream echoed again. I looked around for Sophie but she was gone. The scream forced me off my feet again as I was pushed against the wall, my feet hovering inches from the ground. The force of the scream held me in place. If I got out of this alive, I was for sure going to be deaf.

"Riley!" I called out, but it was useless. My voice was mute against the sound of lightning and a screech in the air. The banshee stopped just long enough for us to get out of the hall. Conner reached for his radio around his belt and yelled into it, but the sound came out dead.

"What the hell is going on?" he shouted.

"Banshee. It's causing a storm inside your station. Where the hell are the other cops?"

"It's a small town, Thomas. There aren't as many of us as you see in the movies. Drew and Kelsey are on traffic."

"And they left you in charge?" Riley asked.

Conner ignored her. "Come on, let's get into the armoury.

Conner led us into what appeared to be a large broom closet but to my surprise it was fairly large. He urged our large crew inside and closed the door. He grabbed Gary by the shoulder and began undoing his handcuffs. Gary was bleeding from somewhere under his shirt. Riley went to him and looked for any way to bandage him up.

"Great," Riley said. "Now we are trapped and there is some sort of monster we can't see trying to kill us. What did we do?"

I ran my hand through my hair. "It doesn't want us. It wants him," I said gesturing to Gary. "It wants to punish him for harming Sophie."

Conner twirled the handcuffs in his finger. "I mean, we could give her what she wants right? Wouldn't that stop it?"

Riley swiped the handcuffs from his hand, pulling his finger back in the process.

He yanked his hand away and cradled it. "Or…we could figure out a way to stop her. Can't Sophie speak to her?" She looked around as if looking for her.

I shook my head. "She isn't here. I think Miss Opera Singer out there harnessed Sophie and is using her energy to make her stronger."

Mr. Hunter slapped the book on the table. "That makes sense. This banshee was weak and has been using Sophie's power for a while now. She has been getting accustomed to how to use her to her advantage. Thomas? Have you noticed per chance Sophie getting stronger over the last few days?" Son of a bitch.

"So here is what we are gonna do," Conner said, banging his hand on the table next to the book. "We are going to stay in here and send Thomas out there to deal with it. He is the one that can speak to the damn thing."

Riley punched him in the arm. "We don't know that for a fact. Stop trying to throw people into the lion's den!"

"I was gonna say graveyard, but lion's den works," said Hunter cheekily.

"Okay, stop this!" I shouted. "We need a plan." Conner opened his mouth to speak but Riley shut him down. "An ACTUAL plan that doesn't involve us going out there and dealing with Mrs Broken Stereo. No offense, Gary."

Gary said nothing. Just leaned against the wall by a light switch.

Conner threw his hands up in defeat. I looked at Mr Hunter who was fiddling with and cleaning his glasses. Riley had her hands on her hips, just staring at me. "Thomas?"

She said, "What IS the plan?"

I breathed heavily. "I gotta stop this. I dragged you all into this, it's my responsibility." I put my hand on the handle of the cold steel door ready to open it before I felt the force of a hand slam it back shut.

Conner stood over me, scowling. "You are not going out into that station unsupervised, freak."

I glared back. "Conner, I have to stop this. I have got to stop the Banshee and protect Sophie before anyone else gets hurt. I'm going."

He applied more pressure to the door. "The hell you are."

"Okay, fine," I said. "You can come with me."

"The hell I am."

Riley hopped over and stood beside me. "If you are going, so am I."

I gave her a worried look. "No, Riley. Not this time."

She looked outright pissed. "Why the hell not? Don't shut me out. Not now. Not after all we've been through."

I looked down at my shoes. "No Riley. I can't lose you. You're the first person to ever see me for me and I am not going to put you in harm's way. Not again." She didn't respond. She just stood there scolding me.

I couldn't look at her. "You ready, Detective?"

Conner's eyes were wild. "You can't be serious? We don't even know what that thing is or what it is capable of!"

I stood straight. "Then I guess it is time we found out."

Mr. Hunter smiled brightly, admiring my turn of character. I had to admit, despite this possibly being my last night on Earth…it did feel pretty good.

Conner pinched his nose. "Fine, but we are not going in blind." He walked over to the nearby light switch and flipped it on. The back wall, which had been dimly lit black till now lit up revealing the armoury for what it really was.

Rifles, shotguns, pistols, a freaking Desert Eagle, and so help me a fucking rocket launcher were all lit up in rows and rows of lights.

I found myself noticing that my jaw had gone slack. I heard Riley mumble something under her breath. It was like a scene out of a spy thriller.

"Take only the light stuff. We gotta move fast," Conner said as he spun two pistols around his fingers like a freaking western and slipped them into his belt. He readied a shotgun over his shoulder and pulled a M16 rifle off the wall. He then began quickly loading each of them carefully and precisely.

"Holy hell," Riley managed to say, with a twinkle in her eye. I gave her a stare that I am sure made me look more foolish than intimidating.

"What? That was hot," she said subtly.

I threw my head back and moaned. "Oh come on guys! This is a freaking ghost, not a zombie of the undead. What the hell do you think bullets are going to do to something that can't be pierced by a physical object?" I shouted.

Conner finished loading his Desert Eagle and spun the cylinder locking it in place. "You know what they say about guns, Casper. I'd rather have it and not need it, than need it and not…"

I slammed my hands on the table. "Oh please. Spare me your cop cliches."

Conner holstered his gun and stepped toward me. "Okay, since you're the expert, what the hell do we bring, huh? Because I am NOT going out there empty handed."

I turned on my heel and eyed the wall of supplies. I pulled down two flashlights and threw one at him. "Really? A flashlight?" I smiled. He hated it.

Riley rummaged through a drawer and pulled out some little baggies with something colorful inside. "Here, at least take these." She threw the bag in my direction and I caught it to check it out. It was a pair of ear plugs, bright orange against my pale skin. I put them in my pocket and nodded an understanding at Riley, who seemed to shrug it off.

I sighed. "I gotta find Sophie. I have to somehow get that…thing to relax long enough to calm it down and…stop it, somehow."

"Thomas, this is suicide," Riley said.

Visions of Simon and his blindsided mistake, of Vinny, my spiritual roommate, and his chance to find kindness and happiness fell upon me, and all the ghosts I'd ever encountered along my many years as an Ectomancer crossed through my mind.

"It just might be," I said to Riley over my shoulder. "But that doesn't stop everybody." I opened the door with Conner on my heel and stepped out into the cold dark hallway ready to face down death.

CHAPTER
SEVENTEEN

THE station looked completely deserted. My footsteps echoed with every step, glass shattering beneath the rubber of my shoe. I looked at the debris all along the stone floor. Picture frames and plaques of all shapes had been crushed by the banshee's forceful scream. Surveying the destruction, every instinct in me told me to turn around and run, but Detective Conner was hot on my trail and I felt the need to impress him.

"You okay back there, Leroy?" I whispered back.

"What?" he said.

I turned around and saw Conner pointing at the ear plug inside his ear. Right. It was gonna be a silent investigation. I gave him a thumbs up as he gripped onto his flashlight tight.

The walls were slick and the ground was demolished. The tiles had been uprooted where we stood and my body froze as I looked over toward the wall I had been pinned to not half an hour ago. I was about to turn and signal Conner to stop but he smashed into me and we fell on top of each other. I yelped loudly as the ear plug was yanked from my ear.

"Watch it. We are trying to be stealthy. You call yourself a cop?"

He shrugged and held his finger up to his lips. He pointed at his eyes and then pointed ahead making some sort of military hand signal, wanting me to follow him. I let him pass by as I fell into step behind him. I hate it when I'm not the hero.

"You…have…mommy…stop."

Sophie? The voice echoed through the shattered halls down the corridor toward us. I grabbed Conner's shoulder to stop him from taking another step. He turned and gave me an angry look that relaxed as he saw the concern in my eyes. Conner looked around the hall as if looking to swap a fly, but it quickly dawned on him how useless it was.

"You see it?" he whispered urgently.

I shook my head. "What's down that way?"

Conner looked to where I was looking. "It's the station's cafeteria. You think our monster wanted a sandwich?"

I rubbed my stomach. "Doubtful. Clearly you have never had prison food."

Conner gave me a distinct look that told me to shut up as he unholstered his pistol. I wanted to remind him of how ineffective that would be, but I was growing tired of the arguing. I know, it surprised me, too.

We clung to the wall as Conner led us along toward the cafeteria entrance. There was a window that looked inside just before the archway that had a sense of horror about it. I urged Conner to crouch down out of sight while I took the lead to investigate. I lurched forward peering around the corner, and I could feel the hair on my arms being pulled by some electrical current. There in the center of the cafeteria stood the Banshee, standing perfectly still. Its body was convulsing as a small ghostly hand was trying to reach out through the monster's belly. That…thing…had somehow devoured Sophie's spirit…and she was fighting to get out.

"Okay, Conner. Here is the plan. I am going to approach it from behind and…" I fell silent. I didn't know what I was going to do. I'd tried to do something as simple as give a ghost a hug and all that happened was I phased through them. I spaced out and I felt my body begin to tremble. To my surprise I felt a sturdy hand touch my shoulder in an act of reassurance.

"Thomas? You good?"

I sighed. "I don't know what we are going to do, Detective."

Conner looked into the cafeteria. "Well, okay. If you say it's in the center, we gotta find a way to mark it, right?"

I looked at him, uncertain. "Yeah, that would certainly help. You have a plan on how to do that?"

I saw Conner surveying the cafeteria. He snapped his fingers and a devil-like smile spread across his face. "I think I do. You said the spirit is in the center of the cafeteria?"

I looked again. "Yeah. It is standing there next to the third table on our right."

"Perfect. Wait here."

My jaw went slack with confusion, but I had to admit I admired his courage. What the hell was he going to do though? He couldn't even see the Banshee, much less fight it.

I watched Conner creep as silently as he could along the cafeteria floor, nearly going into a crawl as he neared the company sink that was stationed under a cabinet of wooden doors. He grabbed the counter and brought himself to his feet as he grabbed the handle of the door and opened it with delicate ease, reaching inside. I strained my eyes to see what he was doing. I looked from him back to the Banshee, who seemed unaware of his actions. I turned just in time to see Conner brandishing a ketchup bottle in his hand pointing it directly at the screaming ghoul. "TAKE THIS!" Conner shouted, holding the ketchup like a garden hose.

The ketchup flew through the air, and for someone who couldn't see what he was shooting at, his aim was right on target. Would have been perfect had the ketchup not gone through the spectre and spattered all over the adjacent table, making it look like a murder scene.

I stepped into the cafeteria. "Conner…WHAT THE FUCK WAS THAT?"

Conner's smile fell into a look of terror. "I…I thought that it would…

"What part of ghost do you not get?"

Suddenly a loud scream erupted from the monsters, flinging us both back up against the wall. Conner dropped the ketchup bottle and darted toward me to the door. I reached out to grab him but the Banshee got there first. It grabbed him and threw him across the cafeteria into a stack of chairs. I ran around the monster toward Conner to help him, but my legs got kicked out from under me. My jaw hit the ground with a rattling jolt. I looked up to see the monster towering over me, its face full of dread and terror, behind those eyes an angry and horrified mother. I tried to listen for Sophie's voice but it was hidden beneath that terrible static that pierced my ears.

I turned my head to look for Conner. He had gotten to his feet and was using the chair for support. He appeared to be trembling. Sophie messing with him had been one thing, but this spectral being had hit him with a much more powerful force. I looked back at the Banshee and for a split second, I could see the look of a beautiful woman, dressed in a night gown who had a look of pure sorrow. It was the look of a woman that had lost her daughter, and would do anything to protect her. The banshee ignored me and darted back toward Conner, her hand reaching out. She gripped Conner by the throat and threw him across the room again up against the cabinet, all the condiments inside being scattered across the floor. Conner stared down at them, wiping blood from his brow.

"Thomas? We need a plan, man. Anything will do at this point."

I didn't know. I was frozen solid. I thought about the cold chill of the Reaper I had encountered. Maybe if we held out long enough he could take care of it? He wanted Sophie's soul right? Was it corrupted being captured inside another? I sure as hell couldn't tell Conner that there was such a thing as the Grim Reaper now. He was barely holding it together as he was with regular ghosts. I rolled on my back and pushed myself back up to my feet to get near Conner. He looked bruised and battered, and yet he still made it look good.

"Well, before you started throwing things at it, it seemed to be calm, and we clearly can't run away from it. What do you think?"

The Banshee began to charge. Its mouth was open wider than humanly possible and its ghostly skin fluttered rapidly behind it. Conner shrugged. "Well, if I am going to die in my place of work, I am not going out without a fight." He picked up more condiments and began throwing them in all directions. "You tell me where the bitch is, okay?"

Conner threw the mustard, the BBQ sauce, and the pepper. The monster got closer and closer at an alarming rate, however this cafeteria was pretty well stocked. He reached down to grab his last bit of 'ammo' and launched it at the feet of the monster. It crashed with a tiny thud as glass slid across the floor, and then a dangerous and powerful shriek went out across the entire room. I covered my ears and closed my eyes tightly as the wailing pierced the air. I could feel my brain frost over like if I had a severe brain freeze. I managed to look at Conner who was experiencing the same thing. I held my breath and waited, knowing that this was going to be my final moments. I, Thomas Crane, was going to know what it was like to be on the other side of the ghost wall.

Bang. Crash. Crunch.

Silence.

There was silence.

I opened my eyes and saw the banshee not three feet from my face. Its eyes were huge and full of anger and pain, and then the heavy breathing started. It struggled and thrashed and flailed before turning around and rushing toward the wall. The soft cry of Sophie called out to me one last time before vanishing into the cold steel. I turned to Conner and gave a slight chuckle as Conner had his head tucked between his knees covering his head.

"Do you see it, Thomas? Did we win?"

I rubbed the back of my neck. "No, I don't think we won, but we scared it off."

Conner slowly got to his feet. "Okay, that's it. We need to get out of here. That was too close."

I frowned. "I'm not going anywhere without Sophie."

Conner turned to look at me. "Look around you, Thomas. We don't know what we are doing! Ghosts are real.

Yes. I believe you! Now how do we stop them? We don't know! Don't you think that is kind of important in this job or am I the crazy one?"

I stopped listening. I was too busy surveying the ground. There, along the broken glass was a solid line of sodium chloride.

"Conner, you are a fucking genius."

Conner stepped up to where I was and looked down at my feet. "Is that…salt?"

I nodded slowly, then turned and bolted for the door. "Come on, we have to get back to the others."

EIGHTEEN

CONNER and I ran into the armoury and I was met by a punch to the arm by Riley.

"Where the hell were you guys? It sounded crazy out there! I was about to head out there and look for you."

"I held her back, don't worry," Mr. Hunter said with his kind smile.

Riley rolled her eyes. "So what's going on? Did you stop it? Where is Sophie?"

I raised my hand to silence her. "It's not over, unfortunately. We had a bit of a scrap. Sophie has been captured and…"

"Is she okay?" Gary was sitting at a table with an empty cup of coffee, looking very defeated. "Did you find my daughter?"

I smiled weakly. "I know where she is, but we have to calm down your wife. Luckily, Detective Numb-nuts here found out Miss. Screamer has a salt allergy."

Detective Conner tried to do his best to look heroic but I don't think he truly knew what he did. "All part of the plan. Right, Crane?"

I looked at Mr. Hunter. "Anything in that book about how salt can stop ghosts?"

Mr. Hunter carried his book over to the table. "I tried to mention it earlier but you seemed rather uninterested. Back in various folklore and fables it is said that salt is often associated with the protection against a ghost or spirit. It is a purifying agent that once…"

"Thanks Professor, but will it stop it?" Conner said tapping his foot.

Mr. Hunter nodded his head. "With enough salt you should be able to hold it in place long enough to talk to it."

I clapped my hands together. "Fantastic." I turned to face Conner. "Okay, so where do you guys keep the salt?"

Conner blinked. "In the cafeteria, but…that was all of it. There isn't any more."

I ran my fingers through my hair, realizing that this seemed to be my own coping mechanism. "What do you mean there is no more salt?"

"I mean that's all of it. This is a prison. Not a food market."

"Great," Riley interjected. "So we're fucked."

Mr. Hunter opened his book and began to skim the pages. "We can't give up yet. Think, everybody. Does anybody know where we can get that much salt?"

The room fell silent as we pondered our predicament.

"The hardware store?" I said at last. "They have bags and bags of the stuff for when it gets icy out."

"Would that even work?" Conner asked. "We know the table salt is effective, but would the rock salt work the same?"

We all looked at Mr. Hunter expectantly. "You don't think there's a section in the books about street salt do you?" he said somewhat irritably. "On one hand, salt is salt and so it should work. On the other hand, we don't know if there are any. additives. So, if the point is to purify that could be problematic. The question is, are you willing to chance it?"

Now, all eyes were on me. "At this moment, it's better than nothing," I said.

Riley piped up, "It's pointless, anyway," she said. "The hardware store is closed."

I looked at Conner, "There's no chance you would look the other why while we. .. "

I began. He stared back stonily. "No, there's not." he said. That put us back at square one, no salt, and we were rapidly running out of time.

I thought and I thought hard. Then those thoughts turned to a headache and I felt my eyes close tightly. So tightly in fact I thought I was going to tear through the skin of my eyelids. The headache turned from pain to dread as I felt the way I did for years every morning before crawling out of bed to my obnoxious alarm clock and my ghostly roommate.

"Damn it. I got to go back to work."

CHAPTER

NINETEEN

"THE Pretzel Shack?" Riley shouted. "You cannot be serious."

Oh, but I was. I knew that shack like the back of my hand. Joe's Twisted Snacks was not just the most toxic place in the entire mall, it was also the saltiest with the worst pretzels in town. Everyone knew it. But it was there, and it was something to eat. And today that crappy pretzel joint was going to save a little girl.

Or kill us trying.

"Riley, Thomas, and I will take the car to the mall," Conner said. "Mr. Hunter, do you think you can take care of Mr. Brownstone?"

Mr. Hunter looked at Gary. He was staring at the wall ominously, his eyes glassed over like he was deep in thought, but looking at nothing.

"Mr. Brownstone? You okay?" I said.

He turned his head slowly and looked at me. No, he looked past me, as if he wasn't looking at me at all. His lips pursed together, as a single breath escaped his lips. He said nothing.

I shook my head. I had enough on my plate than to worry about him being spaced out. I checked the clock on the wall. Not much time left before the Reaper was supposed to come and take away Sophie forever. I had to get her back.

"Come on guys, we are racing the clock," I said.

"What do you mean? What's the rush?" Conner questioned.

I looked at Riley. "We may or may not be racing Death."

Conner looked at me. "That better be a metaphor. What are you not telling me?"

"Death waits for no one," I said. "Not even the dead."

Conner put the key in the ignition and the car sputtered to life. The radio made a static sound that made my heart skip and for a moment I was reminded of when Sophie had possessed the car. I took a breath and explained to Conner to the safest of my abilities about the Reaper and what it planned to do. I needed to stop Sophie's mom from holding her so she could be set free. Conner held the steering wheel tightly, I could tell he was trying to look professional while also trying to understand all the crazy I was spilling out of my mouth. I had a horrible feeling. Were we being followed? I checked behind us through the window and every car made my skin crawl. I was getting paranoid in this vendetta.

"So we have less than two hours to rescue this ghost girl so that her soul can have rest? Seems like a lot of stuff that we have no business dealing with."

Riley touched my arm in the backseat. "We didn't have to get involved, but we choose to. Right, Thomas?"

I looked out the window as the car came to a halt outside the mall. My heart dropped to my stomach as I looked at the front door. Years of my life had gone by in a flash in that

building and after my last talk with my ex-boss I never thought
I would have to step foot inside again.

"Alright. Who wants a snack?" I said.

"Let's get this over with," Riley said. "I don't want to be
here anymore than you."

Conner stretched, getting out of the car. "Let's go
shopping."

I took a glance around the parking lot for any car that
may have been following us, but the lot seemed vacant.

The three of us entered into the mall. It was just as busy
as usual which means there was hardly anyone there. I am sure
to the naked eye we looked like the oddest group to hang out in
the shopping plaza. A cop, a goth rebel, and me, the ghost
whisperer. Okay, maybe not as freaky as some, but not your
typical crowd.

We approached Joe's Twisted Snack shack and to my
misfortune, my old boss Franklin was behind the counter. He
had a large bandage wrapped around his head and his hair was
matted and knotted. He turned from the counter long enough
for me to see his face, his eyes were puffy and he had a look of
discomfort around him. It made me so happy.

"How's it going, boss?" I said cheerfully resting my
elbow on the counter.

Franklin grabbed a rolling pin, I am pretty sure it's the
same one I'd use to give this man a lump the size of my thumb
on the back of his head and pointed it at me. "Get the hell out of
here Crane. You are fired, and above that I have a restraining
order on your ass. So beat it."

I scoffed. "What a shame. All I wanted was a snack."

He tapped the roller on his palm. "Get out of my mall."

Riley reached over the counter and pulled him forward by his shirt. "Listen, Butterbreath. We need all the salt you have behind the counter in the next ten seconds before I hop over this counter and twist your limbs into a pretzel. Do you hear me?"

Franklin squirmed and his face turned sour. "Get off me, you crazy bitch, before I call the cops on you!"

Conner tapped his finger on the counter and displayed his badge. "Just do what the kids say, okay? Police business."

Holy shit. It's true what they say about a man in uniform. I looked at Riley who seemed starstruck. I hate that.

Franklin began to smooth out his shirt. "What is this all about?"

Conner gave me a sideways glance. "It's time for us to put someone to rest."

Franklin turned around and started pulling out bags of salt. "What, you're going to give someone a heart attack?"

Conner started handing bags to Riley and I. "The opposite actually. We are going to help someone to start living."

Franklin rolled his eyes. "This is ridiculous and it's coming out of your paycheck, Thomas."

I smiled. "You know I don't work here anymore. Besides, for once in your life you may actually be doing something right."

"What do you…"

Before I could give him a snappy response, the lights began to sway in the mall and one by one the lights began to crack and shatter above our heads.

I gulped. The lights began to falter and the place grew dim. The mall escalator came to a halt. The electronics department's lights flashed before burning out. All the power in the mall was being sucked up into a single source. The Banshee was in the building.

"How did it follow us from the station?" yelled Conner.

"It must have somehow gotten inside the car on our way over here!" I replied.

"Remind me to start having ghost repellent in the car!" he countered.

"That's if we make it out!" I found myself yelling over the building static sounds surrounding every inch of the plaza. The wind was heavy and the air was cold. Too cold. "Quick, start laying the salt out on the ground! We have to corner it!"

"But where is it?" Riley hollered, the wind getting stronger.

Conner's radio began to frantically act up. "Guys...he got...you have to....stop...run..."

I looked over at him. "Turn it off. It's not helping."

Conner grabbed his radio and flipped it in his hand. "No, this is different. It's coming from the station."

I covered my ears and looked in his direction. "You're getting a call? Right now?"

He nodded. "Come in, over. There is a severe incident at the shopping mall. Do you hear me? Do you copy?"

"He knocked me out....escaped."

My eyes grew wide as I recognized that frantic voice. "Mr. Hunter?"

There was a long moment of silence before the call came through again.

"...angry. It's not him...possession."

Everyone's jaws dropped. Mr. Brownstone had followed us here. The front door to the mall smashed open as a heavy brown boot smashed through the glass. A sturdy man with aged eyes began to march up the center of the mall outlet like a freaking killer robot, pushing anyone in his way clear. Not only was he pushing them, he was launching them with the fury of a wrestler.

I stepped forward, salt bag in hand and began to pour it along Mr. Brownstone's path. "Hurry. Riley! You and Conner begin to pour it around the other side of the hall. I am going to distract it."

Riley looked uncertain. "How are you going to do that?"

I shrugged. "Hey, I am playing this by ear."

Mr. Brownstone got closer and closer and I held my breath as he stepped down inches from the salt. He opened his mouth and a female scream emanated from his mouth. It was cold, harsh and bitter and I could feel my heart in my throat. And then…it spoke through him.

"You have hurt my family. Why?"

I cupped my ears, but spoke as calmly as I could. "I did no such thing. Your daughter is Sophie, right?"

"Mommy, stop this!" Her voice rang from somewhere inside Mr. Brownstone's vessel. "These are my friends!"

The vessel didn't seem to care or understand. "This man, he wasn't there to protect me. He wasn't there to protect her. This drunken fool must pay."

Mr. Brownstone's body convulsed, and began to lift off the ground. Static electricity and lightning shot from his eyes and mouth in a fit of anger, and a spark flew out of a building mist. The lightning took the form of the mother once more and raised her arms to the sky as lightning blasted from her fingertips, followed by her bellowing scream. I was knocked off my feet and went tumbling head over heels up against the pretzel stand, denting the sign. I rubbed the back of my head as I felt the effects of her strength. I looked up just in time to see Riley and Conner being lifted into the air. Riley grasped her neck as she hovered ten feet in the air. Conner too was being lifted but he seemed to be held in a stronger grasp. His arms appeared to be strapped hard to his sides and he seemed like he was having difficulty breathing. Mr. Brownstone took one heavy step toward the salt…and stepped over.

"Fuck!" I heard Riley yell from the sidelines. "Damn it Crane, this isn't working!"

I gritted my teeth. "It must be because she is controlling a solid vessel. We gotta get her to let him go."

"Yeah?" Conner said. "And how do you expect to do that?"

"Working on it." I said. The angry spirit seemed rattled by its own power. I staggered to my feet, and looked back at the towering spirit. Mr. Brownstone seemed frozen in place, his hands outstretched beside him as this towering ghostly ray shone out of his body.

"I tried to help your daughter," I said, looking up at the raging beast. "I tried to help your husband. I am sorry that your family life got so complicated, but your husband tried. No one looks at their daughter the way he does if they didn't love them."

"Lies!" The ghostly woman cried. She raised her hand producing another ray of electricity and launched it at my head. I closed my eyes and waited for the pain. I felt it. But it didn't come from where I expected. I felt a strong force hit me in the side of the arm and I felt myself crashing to the floor in a heap. I looked to my left and saw a smoldering pillar of smoke radiating where I had just been standing. I ran my hand over my body and felt for injuries, but there were none.

I felt something though, but what was it? I felt this overwhelming sense of safety. I felt a sense of compassion. I felt an essence of…power. Then a voice echoed into my head, as if it was standing right next to me in a small but confident voice. "I'll protect you."

Sophie.

I reached my hand out and spread my fingers. A ghostly ray flowed from my shoulder, down my arm, and itched along my fingertips. I could see a ghostly mist spread through my veins and encompass my hand. I turned my wrist and saw a ghostly spiral emanating from the center of my palm. I focussed it on the towering Banshee and a wild grin crossed my face.

"Let…him…go," I said.

The beast roared a scream, but I interrupted it as a force of spiritual energy shot from my hand piercing the banshee in the chest. She wailed and her ghostly body seemed to shake. She shot me a glance of anger and surprise and launched another barrage of lightning strikes at me.

I dipped and jumped behind the trashed pretzel stand, and steadied my hand. What I figured should have been painful, felt cool and eased. My hand shone bright with a ghastly shine of green. I heard the voice in my head again. "Go easy on her. My mommy is upset and needs to calm down."

"Sophie? Where are you?" I asked, looking at my hand.

"I'm here with you, silly," she said softly. "Now let's protect my dad."

I nodded. I leaped over the stand and launched a full blast of ecto-energy from my hand. It left dents around the ghostly shroud of Sophie's mother. I jumped and rolled behind a nearby stand, ready to launch another shot.

"Riley? Conner? You guys okay?" I yelled from behind my cover.

"Hmmph. Grummppphhh…" I heard them both say in some various forms.

"Yeah, I assumed as much. Hold on."

I shot another ecto blast and the banshee screamed in pain as it pelted against her. She reached out a ghostly hand toward me and I felt a tug. Sophie began to leave me. She gripped onto my aura and clung tight.

"Sophie!" I shouted. I reached out and felt my hand touch hers. A physical touch. A STRONG touch. I gripped her hand and pulled her back into my chest before putting my palms together and channeling the biggest ecto shot I could, but this time, I aimed it at Gary.

"Sorry, Mr. Brownstone. This might hurt," I muttered, mostly to myself.

I released my energy and the shot hit him square in the torso. He fell over backwards, hard and fast. His eyes shone bright for the first time in a while as the spectre left him. She screamed and howled as she lost her tether, and Riley and Conner fell from her grasp.

"Conner, now!" I shouted.

"Ow…" said Conner, rubbing the back of his head. He reached out and grabbed the bag of salt and slung it across the floor to Riley. Riley had landed on her feet and was already on the run pouring the salt into a circle. "Ready when you are, Thomas!" she shouted.

I grabbed Mr. Brownstone's leg and pulled him across the floor, and completed the circle. The banshee was stuck in a large ring of salt, and she was raging.

"Okay, Mrs. Brownstone," I said. "It's time for you to go to bed." I raised my hand, channeled all my energy and then… Nothing.

I stood there looking surprised. I turned my hand around and the green spectral energy had faded away. I looked from my hand to the beast who was staring at me with sadness, and anger.

"Don't hurt her," a tiny voice said.

Sophie appeared before me. She didn't look at me, but she was staring hard at her mother. The banshee outstretched her hands and Sophie took a step forward but did not approach her.

"I know how I died, mommy. And it's okay," she said calmly.

I stood next to Sophie. "You did everything you could. It is not your fault, nor is it your husband's. You tried to save her, just like a good mother should."

"I love my family," The wailing voice said. It sounded eerie, but sincere. "I just wanted us to be together again."

"One day you will," I said. I thought of Simon, and his sacrifice. It had brought him loneliness and sadness, and an eternity to think of how he could fix it. "You can't rush compassion. You must be there for the ones you love. Through life…and death."

"I will always love you," I heard a voice say. I turned and Gary had gotten to his feet and was looking at his wife, tears in his eyes. "I will always be there for you." Sophie smiled and ran up, hugging her father. He rested his hand upon the shoulder of his ghostly daughter.

"I love you daddy," Sophie said. "I'll always be there for you."

Sophie turned and took a step toward her mother before turning around and hugging me. "Thank you for protecting me. You really do have a kind heart."

I fought back tears of my own. "Uhh…Thank you Sophie. You…you take care now."

She smiled up at me. "We make quite the team, huh?"

I nodded. "Yeah, about that. How were you able to…you know…" I showed her my hand.

She laughed at me. "Silly. I used your energy. What? You don't feel it?"

I thought about that for a minute. How was she able to see it? How was she able to join with it? How did she know?

"Sophie…how?"

She laughed again. "Watch this." She took my hand and closed her eyes. A white light floated from her forehead and placed itself upon my palm. The spectral green mist returned, brighter and stronger than ever.

"It is part of my soul, Thomas. I want you to have it. For helping me."

I blinked. Part of her soul had given me the ability to do those crazy light tricks that had stopped her mother.

"Sophie…how did you…how…?"

She giggled. "Looks like you have some work to do, mister."

I smiled. "Yeah, I guess I do."

The room suddenly began to grow cold, and a dark mist embodied everyone in the room. I held my breath as a boney figure in a black hood formed in front of me, standing tall and with pride.

"It is time, Mr. Crane," he bellowed.

I took a step forward. "No. I'm not ready. There has to be another way to save her."

The Reaper bowed his head and gave me a look of certainty. "You have done so much, Thomas. More than most in your position would ever do. The one they call Sophie will be safe, and she will have safe passage to the other side."

I looked at Sophie who was fighting tears while holding onto the large female spectre. "And what of her mother?"

The Reaper bowed his head. "She will be punished for manipulating the spirit realm, but she will be safe to see her daughter as she pleases. We spirits are not so easily detoured."

I looked at him, uncertain but for once I knew it unsafe to reply. I gave him a stern nod.

The Reaper smiled a boney smile. "I will see you again."

Sophie turned away as the Reaper touched her shoulder. "Thomas, help those that need you. Your soul is too kind to let them stay lost." She then motioned to Riley who was standing off, looking at me. "And not just the ghost ones, either." She winked at me.

I felt the strong, sturdy hand of Mr. Brownstone on my shoulder. He nodded at his family, smiling. "I'll see you again one day. I promise."

With that final word, Sophie and her mother vanished in a pool of green light as the Reaper waved his hand. They were gone in a smokey flash that sent a final chill through the air. I turned to face Mr. Brownstone who stood at the wall with a loving expression.

I turned and saw Riley and Conner staring at me. Riley quickly wiped away a tear, smiling at me. "Mr. Brownstone, I am sorry if I interfered or anything…"

He shook his head. "Sir, there are no words to express how thankful I am that you came into my daughter's life. You convinced not only your friends, but myself that I am not crazy. I can't thank you enough."

I shook my head. "This…ability we share, there is so much to it that we don't understand. Maybe if we…"

He raised his hand, silencing me. "No. I'm done. I have this ability and it made me lose the thing I care about most in this world. I do not wish to touch it again." He looked at me, with wisdom in his eyes. "But you…I think you might still be able to do some good with it."

I stared at my hand, channeling my energy. I created a small orb of mist between my fingers. "Maybe I can."

Mr. Brownstone stared at the floating orb and heaved a heavy sigh. "Of all the souls to help you become stronger, I hope she helps you as much as she helped me."

I choked back tears of my own. "Mr. Brownstone, come with us back to town and we can…"

"I appreciate the offer, friend, but I am going to stay here for a while longer. Say goodbye to my family. If you ever need anything, don't be afraid to ask, okay?"

I nodded and shook his hand. "Anytime."

CHAPTER

TWENTY

CONNER and Riley came up behind me. "So…you're going to clean up this mess or what?" said Conner.

"In your dreams, Conner," I said. "I am curious…how do you plan on reporting this? Are you ready to tell the small city in Indiana that ghosts are real?"

Conner put his hands on his hips and surveyed the destroyed mall. "Well, they are not going to believe that. Maybe I'll just say a bear did it."

"A supernatural bear," Riley said with her eyes wide.

"Something like that."

From somewhere under some debris a shrill voice came from the shadows.

"My shop! Who the hell is going to pay for this? Thomas? Oh you are going to be selling pretzels for the rest of your life!"

"You fired me, remember? Besides, I am sure someone will cover it. Like, the person in charge? You have insurance?"

Franklin's face could not have looked more angry. "Crane, I am going to kill you."

I smiled back at him. "Try it, I hear the afterlife is actually pretty bad ass."

Riley took my hand. "Yeah, Franklin. Don't be so salty."

Conner rolled his eyes. "A pun? Really?"

I smiled. "Come on guys. Let's get out of here."

Franklin continued to swear and curse as we exited the mall, the broken glass doors closing behind us.

*   *   *

WE arrived back at my apartment as the sun began to set. The police cruiser sat with the three of us sitting in silence. Conner was the first to exit the vehicle and stood with his arms crossed leaning on the stairwell to my apartment complex's front door.

"So..." Riley said. "How much trouble do you think we are gonna get in?"

I looked at my hand, still trying to piece together everything. "I guess we better find out."

Riley got out of the car and stepped onto the sidewalk. I opened my door, but I didn't move. Conner began to tap his foot.

"You in some sort of rush, Detective?"

He glared at his feet. "Well, I did just have a mindblowing case that changed my perspective of the world, so pardon me for feeling antsy."

Riley stepped up to him and eyed him up and down. "You know, you are not like other cops I have tangled with."

Conner gave her a glance. "No?"

Riley smiled. She leaned forward and kissed his cheek. Conner placed his hand upon it and smiled back at her, winking. I felt an overwhelming sense of jealousy wash over me.

"You know," he said. "I really should turn you in for…well, a long list of crimes you committed over the last few days."

"That so?" Riley said, flirtatiously. "Guess you better keep a closer eye on me, huh?"

"I guess I will." Riley, flipped her beautiful hair, and her short skirt swished back and forth as she pranced back over to the car, blushing. Damn it.

Conner stepped toward me as I sat in the back of the car. I fought the urge to not attack him.

"So, Thomas. You and I have some things to discuss, don't we?"

I shuddered. "You gonna kiss me too and let me go?"

He smiled. "Not my type, Thomas. Look, I know we saw some things today that no one is going to see or believe or want to believe, and because of that I am not going to tell them."

I gave him a weary look. "So what are you going to do?"

He brushed his hair back. "I am a detective, Crane. I'll weave a story. You know…" He bit his lip as if contemplating what he wanted to say next. "You have a gift that could seriously come in handy in the police force. You ever think of joining?"

I blinked up at him. "Are you seriously offering me a job?"

He scraped his boot along the curb. "Don't get carried away. You are much too squishy for this line of work. But, where there is one ghost there ought to be many more. Perhaps you can work with us as a consultant? Help us with this and that?"

"You are offering me a job?" I repeated.

He reached into his pocket and handed me a card with his number on it.

"You need one, don't you?" He winked at me. Damn it, he was good.

I rose to my feet as I got out of the car and gave him a handshake. "Thank you. For believing in me."

"I never doubted you for a second," he joked. He turned and gave Riley a nod that said call me and got back into the police car. He rolled down the window and waved at me. "Hey freak, stay out of trouble, you hear?"

I waved back as the car revved up and drove off down the street. Riley stood beside me as we watched his car turn from view. I felt her eyes on me, but I didn't want to look at her. I didn't want to feel that jealousy again.

"I am so proud of you, Thomas," she said,

"I didn't do much. Just helped a little girl find her family."

Riley punched my arm. "That's more than most do."

I rubbed my arm. "Yeah, I guess so."

She leaned around me to try and look at my face. "Hey, we just saved the town, and you're moping? You did a cop gig and now you're the master of brooding? What is wrong?"

I gave her a look that for whatever reason made her take a step back. "Riley, you and I have been through so much together and you...I have always...I thought..."

She looked down at the street, as if realizing what I was going to say. She reached into her back pocket and brandished a cigarette. She offered me one, but this time, I didn't take it.

"You're a weird guy," she said, "And I will always admire that most about you." She lit the smoke and stared off down the road. "I don't get close to people, Thomas. Never have, never will. You know my favorite part about working at that hell hole is?"

I looked at her and waited.

"It's this. These moments here. Where we can talk and share in each other's company. I have never had that, and now that you are gone it's going to…"

She took another huff of her cigarette and looked away. "I am going to miss your freak ass."

I smiled. "You know, we can still hang out, right? Riley, I have always cherished and admired you and there is no one I would rather save the world with, than you."

She turned and smiled at me. "Life is short, huh? Guess it is nice to know that when I die, I'll be around to do whatever I feel like right?"

I nudged her. "There is a lot we don't understand, but one thing is certain, I will always care about you."

She narrowed her eyes at me and smiled. "Right back at you."

She flicked her cigarette on the ground and kissed my cheek. She turned on her heel and walked away, her skirt swishing in the breeze showing off those damn legs.

"I'll see you around, Crane, catch you later, or in the next life."

"See you later, Riley…" I watched her go down the road and round the corner into a nearby alley.

"I love you," I whispered.

EPILOGUE

I stormed up the steps of my apartment building, feeling all kinds of emotions. Anger, happiness, sadness, and confusion were flooding my brain. I needed an energy drink…no, I needed alcohol.

Alcohol…shit. I bolted up the rest of the steps and threw open my door quickly.

"Hey, lad," I heard a voice say. "I was beginning to wonder what had happened to you. You doing okay?"

"Not now, Vinny, I gotta check on something."

Vinny watched as I frantically ran to charge up my phone. It had been dead for days. "You know you have a visitor that has been wanting to talk to you?" he continued.

I tried to ignore him. "Not now, this is important."

"But…"

"It can wait, Vinny," I said. I plugged my phone up and immediately called Mr. Hunter's shop. It rang once before someone answered.

"The Open Page, Hunter speaking."

"Oh thank God you're okay," I said, exasperated.

"Thomas? That you?" he said eagerly.

"Hey man, how are you feeling?"

He hesitated a moment before answering. "I'll be okay. Took a wallop to the head from behind but I think I will be okay. Been doing a lot of studying in my library lately, and

Thomas, I think you need to understand something." I felt myself swallow hard.

"Yeah?"

I could hear a lot of books shuffling in the background. "I got off the phone with the detective earlier and he said that you fused your soul with Sophie's?"

I sat down on my couch. "Yeah. It was the only way to stabilize her mother."

I heard Mr. Hunter breathe heavily. "She may have advanced your ectomancy skills to a powerful degree," he said.

"Hell yeah, she did, I gotta admit it was awesome."

I heard the concern in his voice. "You may want to be mindful of that ability. When she fused her soul with yours, she jumpstarted your ability to perform acts that are otherworldly. If you continue to use that ability too much, you will be using parts of your own soul that will dangerously alter your life."

I closed my eyes and cursed silently. "So you're saying, if I use this ability too much…"

"Poof," he replied.

"Great talk, Doc. I'll keep that in mind." I pinched the bridge of my nose, pulling my hand away quickly as I saw what I was doing. Damn it "Hey, Hunter, I am glad you're okay."

"You too. You take care of yourself and mind what I told you."

I hung up the phone, more aggressively than I meant and leaned back against the couch. I looked at my hand and focused my energy. The green mist foamed up and slowly formed into a ghastly ball of ecto. I cradled it in my hand and carefully made it glide over my palm. "Take care of them, Thomas," Sophie had said.

"I will Sophie," I said aloud. "Or I will die trying."

"Are you going to tell me what is going on?" Vinny said as he came into the room. He stared at my hand and looked confused. "New trick?"

I stood up. "Something like that."

He floated across the room and hovered in front of my face. "Your abilities are growing. I bet you're…"

"They are…" I interrupted. "And I have got to get it under control."

Vinny groaned. "Yes, and you know who may be able to help you?"

I slipped on my black vest and sported my long coat that I thought made me look spiffy and walked toward the door. "I gotta go somewhere where I can figure this stuff out. I am going to the book store to talk to Hunter, maybe then I'll…"

"You always were really good at jumping before looking."

I grabbed the doorknob and gripped it tightly. "Vinny, I don't have time for this right now. I really have to…"

"It wasn't me, chap," Vinny said, defensively. "I told you that you had a visitor."

I opened my eyes wide. That voice did sound familiar but it wasn't Vinny. I knew that voice. Where did I know that voice? I turned around and in front of me spotted a ghost, a little taller than me, with a thick black mustache and dark hair much like mine. He gave me a friendly smile as he looked me up and down. My eyes grew large and my jaw went slack. I tried to get all my emotions under control and everything that had just happened escaped my memory. Standing in my living room was a face I had not seen since…since…

Bang.

"You're…you're my…" Crash.

"Thomas," the ghost said. "Son, your mother is in serious danger, and I am going to need your help."

Crunch.

ACKNOWLEDGEMENTS

Ectomancer: Soul Searcher comes from a special place in my heart. It invites the possibilities that any dream can be reality, as long as you strive for it. It's never easy. It's challenging. And you can make it yours. I was struggling with who I was. I felt my life had become monotonous, until an incredible publishing house reminded me that my creativity wasn't gone, it was just buried.

I had started Ectomancer years ago during the pandemic, just as a way to pass the time. Once work began again, I shelved it and never thought of it again. Line by Lion had the shovel to dig up my crazy ideas and bring them to light for all to see.

I want to thank my parents for always encouraging my imagination to exceed possibilities, and I want to thank my closest friends for tolerating it.

An added thanks to the Renaissance faire community for opening up a world of possibilities. I wouldn't have been half the man I am today if not for their encouraging antics.

A very special thanks to Amanda Lamkin for believing in me and making this possible, and Liz Minton for never giving up on me and encouraging my frantic mind.

Please read ahead for a sneak peek of the sequel, Ectomancer: Deadlift

PROLOGUE

"My mother is WHERE?"

My father crossed his arms, and hovered over in the corner of the bedroom. Vinny stared at him, his mouth dropped, his eyes moving rapidly from me to him.

"Your mother is dying in a mental ward and has been for many years," my father said, looking down at the ground. "I have been watching over her, but I fear there is not much more I can do."

I stared at him furiously. "You don't call. You don't write. You know what I am capable of, or else you wouldn't be here. So why now, huh? Why come to me now that I am finally getting my life under control?

Vinny raised his hand, extending his finger. "Actually, I wouldn't say your life is under – "

"Shut it, Vinny," I said without even looking at him. I was too busy staring daggers into my deceased father's tired eyes. "So why?"

My father's eyes welled up and he turned his attention to my wall. "You don't have many pictures up."

I felt my breathing intensify as my patience dwindled. "I like to keep a clean space."

I could see the edges of my father's cheeks flinch as he attempted a smile. "You don't wish to remember, do you? Remember what our family once was?"

My wrists were numb. I had not noticed my nails digging into my palms so fiercely. "I feel I suffer enough living with death every day of my life."

This time my father did laugh. "You think you are living with death?" he asked. "Try being dead; it's a whole other game."

I took a step towards him. I knew punching a ghost would do no good, but man did I have the urge. I could feel my new ecto powers fueling my veins. "Why are you here, *Mr. Crane*?" I hissed the name as spitefully as I could. Even I was taken aback at how cruel it sounded.

He turned back to me, visible shock on his face. "So I guess we are refraining from father now?"

I clenched my jaw. "You haven't been my father in a long time. .. *sir*."

He bit his lip. "Very well. Then in that case, I will ask you this as a man asking another for help." He glided over to my bedroom desk and sat in the chair very elegantly. "Mr. Crane. I politely ask that you help my wife, who is in dire need of assistance."

I walked across to the opposite side of the room, and sat on my bed. I put my hands together and tried to look composed. It wasn't working.

"What happened to my mother?"

He sighed heavily. "The crash was not kind to her."

"Yeah, no shit." I crossed my arms and felt my foot tapping impatiently. He didn't seem to mind. I could see Vinny in the corner of my eye getting nervous.

"After the crash, your mother was taken away to a medical ward in Shadyville, Indiana. She was spouting what the doctors considered to be nonsense. Saying that her family was alive, that she desperately needed to see you. They considered her mentally unstable because she kept saying she could feel her family's presence. She refused to believe that she lost everything that day."

"But she hadn't," I argued, "I was still alive."

He raised his hand to silence me. "It was unclear. You were badly hurt, and in a very deep coma. They felt it best to send you somewhere else to get examined."

I closed my eyes. "So, it's your fault I haven't seen her since I was a child."

He stared at me seriously. "I had been deceased all of 10 seconds, son. I wasn't exactly a pro. All I knew was that I. .. needed to be near her."

I opened my eyes but didn't' look at him. I didn't want to understand nor did I want to be on his side, but I got it. If I was that close to someone, I wouldn't want to be away from them either."

"When I die, don't leave me stuck on this plane."

Riley's voice was still fresh and haunting in my brain. If I was given a chance, I would do anything to be in her presence as well.

"So, what do you need me to do?"

He smiled weakly. "She is dying, but not due to her illness. I fear a greater power is slowly draining her body."

"Like what? Some act of God?" Vinny chimed.

My father shook his head. "God wouldn't drain her soul the way hers is being taken."

I blinked. "Wait. .. her soul is being drained?"

My father nodded, "I fear it is the work of something evil, and. . . I need help finding out what. Your mother. .. she is too good of a person to suffer like this."

I stood up and went to my closet. I flung open the door, and looked at my rail of disarrayed black clothing from left to right. A single sleeve stood out, leather among the cheap fabric. I pushed the clothes down the line, and pulled out a leather jacket that I had had since I was very young. A gift from my very own mother.

"One of these days you will grow into it. You will be so dashing, and you will lift so many spirits." Her voice sounded beautifully melodic in my head.

"Oh mom, if you only knew," I said to myself.

I slipped into the jacket. It fit me like a glove. I hugged myself briefly, smelling leather and the slightest scent of my mother. I could feel the two ghosts in the room staring at me. I knelt down and rummaged through the closet, and pulled out my large green suitcase. I flung it across the room onto the bed and began pulling out a few shirts.

"What do you think you are doing?" Vinny asked, hands on his hips.

I continued throwing clothes across the room. "I am going to get my mother out of there."

"But you don't even know what is happening to her!"

"It's doesn't matter," my father interjected. "He's a Crane, and Crane's do anything to help their family."

This made me stop. Family. I had kind of forgotten what that word meant. I had been without one for so long, Vinny was the closest thing to family that I could think of.

And Conner, Mr. Hunter, Riley. ..

Sophie.

I held my breath before released a long, drawn out sigh. I had family, and it went far beyond any sort of bloodline. I walked to the bed, threw the clothes into the suitcase, and snapped it shut. I checked my phone, which was still low on battery, and dialed the only person I knew that could help me.

"Mr. Hunter? I'm going to need you to help me get out of town."

"Why? What's wrong? What the hell are you doing?" the static voice replied over the speaker.

I turned to face the spectres in my room, glancing down at my hand as the ecto powers moved effortlessly up my arm, turning my veins a translucent green hue. I grinned my most wolfish grin and spoke firmly into the phone. "I'm going to break into the Shelbyville Med Facility."